"Years ago, Mr. Saroyan postulated that there are two kinds of writers: those who run to meet death, and those who fight to keep it off. It's always been clear which side he's on, and so every person he's met, everything he's done, becomes cause for celebration. . . . He is worth reading . . . because at base, and solid, is the story."
—Joel Oppenheimer, *The New York Times Book Review*

"He achieves the feat of making and keeping us boozy without the use of alcohol and purely by the action of art."
—Edmund Wilson

"Saroyan's stories are part of the permanent literature . . . and his 'country'—particularly San Francisco, Fresno, and their environs—is as real in its way as Faulkner's Mississippi."
—William Peden, author of *The American Short Story: Continuity and Change*

"To recognize the world for what it is, to admit the apparent hopelessness of an affirmation of the individual, yet still to be willing to gamble on human dignity because of the value of the attempt itself sounds more like courage than romanticism."
—Thelma Shinn, *Modern Drama*

WILLIAM SAROYAN

The Human Comedy

REVISED BY THE AUTHOR

A DELL BOOK

Published by
Dell Publishing
a division of
Random House, Inc.

The trademark Dell® is registered in the U.S. Patent and Trademark Office

ISBN: 0-440-33933-2

Reprinted by arrangement with Harcourt Brace Jovanovich, Inc.

Printed in the United States of America

Published simultaneously in Canada

September 1966

70 69 68 67
BVGM

THIS STORY IS FOR

Takoohi Saroyan

*I have taken all this time to write a story especially for
you because I have wanted it to be an especially good story,
the very best I might ever be able to write, and now at
last, a little pressed for time, I have tried. I might have
waited longer still, but as there is no telling what's next or
what skill or inclination will be left after everything else,
I have hurried a little and taken a chance on my present
skill and inclination. Soon, I hope, someone wonderful
will translate the story into Armenian, so that it will be in
print you know well. In translation the story may read
better than it does in English, and, as you have done before, maybe you will want to read some of it to me, even
though I wrote the stuff in the first place. If so, I promise
to listen, and to marvel at the beauty of our language, so
little known by others and so much less appreciated by
anyone than by you. As you cannot read and enjoy English
as well as you read and enjoy Armenian, and as I cannot
read or write Armenian at all, we can only hope for a
good translator. One way or another, though, this story is
for you. I hope you like it. I have written it as simply as
possible, with that blending of the severe and the light-
hearted which is especially yours, and our family's. The
story is not enough, I know, but what of that? It will
surely seem enough to you, since your son wrote it and
meant so well.*

WILLIAM SAROYAN
SAN FRANCISCO, 1942

The Human Comedy

Contents

1. Ulysses

THE LITTLE BOY named Ulysses Macauley one day stood over the new gopher hole in the backyard of his house on Santa Clara Avenue in Ithaca, California. The gopher of this hole pushed up fresh moist dirt and peeked out at the boy, who was certainly a stranger but perhaps not an enemy. Before this miracle had been fully enjoyed by the boy, one of the birds of Ithaca flew into the old walnut tree in the backyard and after settling itself on a branch broke into rapture, moving the boy's fascination from the earth to the tree. Next, best of all, a freight train puffed and roared far away. The boy listened, and felt the earth beneath him tremble with the moving of the train. Then he broke into running, moving (it seemed to him) swifter than any life in the world.

When he reached the crossing he was just in time to see the passing of the whole train, from locomotive to caboose. He waved to the engineer, but the engineer did not wave back to him. He waved to five others who were with the train, but not one of them waved back. They might have done so, but they didn't. At last a Negro appeared leaning over the side of a gondola. Above the clatter of the train, Ulysses heard the man singing:

"Weep no more my lady, O weep no more today
We will sing one song for the old Kentucky home
For the old Kentucky home far away"

Ulysses waved to the Negro too, and then a wondrous and unexpected thing happened. *This* man, black and different from all the others, waved back to Ulysses, shouting: "Going home, boy—going back where I belong!"

The small boy and the Negro waved to one another until the train was almost out of sight.

Then Ulysses looked around. There it was, all around him, funny and lonely—the world of his life. The strange, weed-infested, junky, wonderful, senseless yet beautiful world. Walking down the track came an old man with a rolled bundle on his back. Ulysses waved to this man too, but the man was too old and too tired to be pleased with a small boy's friendliness. The old man glanced at Ulysses as if both he and the boy were already dead.

The little boy turned slowly and started for home. As he moved, he still listened to the passing of the train, the singing of the Negro, and the joyous words: "Going home, boy—going back where I belong!" He stopped to think of all this, loitering beside a china-ball tree and kicking at the yellow, smelly, fallen fruit of it. After a moment he smiled the smile of the Macauley people—the gentle, wise, secret smile which said *Hello* to all things.

When he turned the corner and saw the Macauley

house, Ulysses began to skip, kicking up a heel. He tripped and fell because of this merriment, but got to his feet and went on.

His mother was in the yard, throwing feed to the chickens. She watched the boy trip and fall and get up and skip again. He came quickly and quietly and stood beside her, then went to the hen nest to look for eggs. He found one. He looked at it a moment, picked it up, brought it to his mother and very carefully handed it to her, by which he meant what no man can guess and no child can remember to tell.

2. Homer

His brother Homer sat on the seat of a second-hand bicycle which struggled bravely with the dirt of a country road. Homer Macauley wore a telegraph messenger's coat which was far too big and a cap which was not quite big enough. The sun was going down in a somnolence of evening peace deeply cherished by the people of Ithaca. All about the messenger orchards and vineyards rested in the old, old earth of California. Even though he was moving along swiftly, Homer was not missing any of the charm of the region. Look at that! he kept saying to himself of earth

and tree, vine and sun and cloud. Look at that, will you?
He began to make decorations with the movements of his
bike and, to accompany these ornaments of movement, he
burst out with a shouting of music—simple, lyrical and ridiculous. The theme of this opera was taken over in his
mind by the strings of an orchestra, then supplemented by
the harp of his mother and the piano of his sister Bess.
And finally, to bring the whole family together, an accordion came into the group, saying the theme with an easy
humor, as Homer remembered his brother Marcus.

Homer's music fled before the hurrying clatter of three
incredible objects moving across the sky. The messenger
looked up at the airplanes and promptly rode into a small
dry ditch. A farmer's dog came swiftly and with great importance, barking like a man with a message. Homer ignored the message, turning only once to spoof the animal
by saying "Arp, Arp!" He seated himself on the bicycle
again and rode on.

When he reached the beginning of the residential district
of the city, he passed a sign without reading it:

ITHACA, CALIFORNIA
EAST, WEST—HOME IS BEST
WELCOME, STRANGER

He stopped at the next corner to watch a long line of
Army trucks full of soldiers roll by. He saluted the men,
just as his brother Ulysses had waved to the engineer and
the hobœs. A great many soldiers returned the messenger's
salute. Why not? What did they know about anything?

3. At the Telegraph Office

IT WAS EVENING in Ithaca when Homer finally drew up in front of the telegraph office. The clock in the window said two minutes past seven. Inside the office Homer saw Mr. Spangler, the manager of the telegraph office, counting the words of a telegram which a tired-looking, troubled young man of twenty or so had just handed him. As he came into the office, Homer listened to Mr. Spangler and the young man.

"Fourteen words collect," Spangler said.

"How long will it take the telegram to get to my mother?" the boy said.

"Well, it's pretty late in the East now. It's not easy to raise money late at night sometimes, but I'll rush the telegram right through." Without looking at the boy again, Spangler went through his pockets, coming out with a handful of small coins, one piece of currency and a hardboiled egg.

"Here," he said, "just in case." He handed the boy the currency. "You can pay me back when your mother sends the money." He indicated the egg. "I picked it up in a bar seven days ago. Brings me luck."

The boy looked at the money, astonished. "Thanks," he said, and hurried out of the office.

Spangler took the telegram over to William Grogan, the night-shift telegraph operator and wire-chief. "Send it paid, Willie. I'll pay for it myself."

Mr. Grogan put his hand around the "bug" and began rattling off the telegram in the Morse code, letter by letter:

MRS. MARGARET STRICKMAN
1874 BIDDLE STREET
YORK, PENNSYLVANIA

DEAR MA. PLEASE TELEGRAPH THIRTY DOLLARS. WANT TO COME HOME. AM FINE. EVERYTHING O.K.

JOHN

Homer Macauley studied the delivery desk to see what was on hand for delivery, or if there were any calls to take. Mr. Spangler watched him a moment and then said, "How do you like being a messenger?"

"How do I *like* it?" Homer said. "I like it better than anything. You sure get to see a lot of different people. You sure get to go to a lot of different places."

"Yes, you do," Spangler said. He paused to look at the boy a little closer. "How did you sleep last night?"

"Fine," Homer said. "I was pretty tired but I slept fine."

"Did you sleep a little at school today?"

"A little."

"What subject?"

"Ancient history."

"What about sports? I mean what about not being able to take part in them on account of having this job?"

"I take part in them. We have a physical education period every day."

"Is that so? I used to run the two-twenty low hurdles when I went to Ithaca High. Valley Champion." The manager of the telegraph office paused, then went on. "You really like this job, don't you?"

"I'm going to be the best messenger this office ever had."

"O.K. But don't kill yourself. Get there swiftly, but don't go *too* fast. Be polite to everybody—take your hat off in elevators, and above all things don't lose a telegram."

"Yes, sir."

"Working nights is different from working days. Taking a telegram to Chinatown at night, or out to the sticks, is liable to scare a fellow—well, don't let it scare *you*. People are people. Don't be afraid of them. How old are you?"

Homer gulped. "Sixteen."

"Yes, I know," Spangler said. "You said that yesterday. We're not supposed to hire a boy unless he's at least sixteen, but I thought I'd take a chance on you. How old are you?"

"Fourteen."

"Well, you'll be sixteen in two years, at any rate."

"Yes, sir."

"If anything comes up that you don't understand, come to me."

"Yes, sir," Homer said. He paused. "What about singing telegrams?"

"You've got a pretty good voice, haven't you?"

"I used to sing at the First Presbyterian Sunday School."

"That's fine. That's exactly the kind of voice we need for our singing telegrams. Now, let's say Mr. Grogan over there was sent a birthday greeting. How would you do it?"

Homer went over to Mr. Grogan and sang:

> Happy birthday to you—
> Happy birthday to you—

> Happy birthday, dear Grogan—
> Happy birthday to you.

"Thank you," Mr. Grogan said.

"That's fine," Spangler said to Homer, "but you wouldn't say 'dear Grogan,' you'd say 'dear *Mr.* Grogan.' What are you going to do with the fifteen dollars a week?"

"Give it to my mother."

"All right. From now on you're working—*steady*. You're part of this outfit. Watch things—listen carefully—keep your eyes and ears open." The manager of the telegraph office looked away at nothing a moment and then said, "What future have you mapped out for yourself?"

"Future?" Homer said. He was a little embarassed because all his life, from day to day, he had been busy mapping out a future, even if it was only a future for the next day. "Well," he said, "I don't know for sure, but I guess I'd like to be somebody some day."

"You will be," Spangler said. "Know where Chatterton's Bakery is on Broadway? Here's a quarter. Go get me two day-old pies—apple, and coconut cream. Two for a quarter."

"Yes, sir," Homer said. He caught the quarter Spangler tossed, and ran out of the office. Spangler turned to the telegraph operator and said, "What do you think of him?"

"He's a good boy," Mr. Grogan said.

"Comes from a good, poor family on Santa Clara Avenue. No father. Brother in the Army. Mother works in the packinghouses in the summer. Sister goes to State College. He's a couple of years underage, that's all."

"I'm a couple overage," Mr. Grogan said. "We'll get along."

Spangler did a little work at his desk, and then suddenly got up. "If you want me, I'll be at Corbett's. Share the pies between you—" He stopped and stared, dumbfounded, as Homer came running into the office with two wrapped-up pies.

"What's your name again?" Spangler almost shouted at the boy.

"Homer Macauley."

The manager of the telegraph office put his arm around
the new messenger. "All right, Homer Macauley. You're
the boy this office needs on the night-shift. You're probably
the fastest-moving thing in the San Joaquin valley. You're
going to be a great man some day, too—if you live. So
see that you do." He turned and left the office while
Homer tried to understand the meaning of what the man
had said.

"All right, my boy," Mr. Grogan said, "the pies."

Homer put the pies on the desk beside Mr. Grogan, who
continued to talk. "Homer Macauley, my name is William
Grogan. I am called Willie, however, although I am sixty-
seven years old. I am an old-time telegrapher, one of the
last in the world. I am also night wire-chief of this office. I
am also hungry. Let us feast together on these pies—the
apple and the cocoanut cream. From now on, you and I
are friends."

"Yes, sir," Homer said.

The old telegraph operator broke one of the pies into
four parts, and they began to eat cocoanut cream.

"I shall, on occasion, ask you to run an errand for me,
to join me in song, or to sit and talk to me. In the event of
drunkenness, I shall expect of you a depth of understanding one may not expect from men past the age of
twelve. How old are you?"

"Fourteen, but I've got a pretty good understanding."

"Very well, I'll take your word for it. Every night in this
office I shall count on you to see that I shall be able to per-
form my duties. A splash of cold water in the face if I do
not respond when shaken—this to be followed by a cup of
hot black coffee from Corbett's."

"Yes, sir."

"On the street, however, the procedure is quite another
thing. If you behold me wrapped in the embrace of alcohol, greet me as you pass, but make no reference to my
happiness. I am a sensitive man and prefer not to be the
object of public solicitude."

"Cold water and coffee in the office," Homer said.
"Greeting in the street. Yes, sir."

The telegraph box rattled. Mr. Grogan answered the call

and took his place at the typewriter, but went on talking. "I believe I overheard you say that once upon a time you sang at Sunday School. Please be good enough to sing one of the Sunday School songs you know while I type this message from Washington, D. C."

Homer sang *Rock of Ages* while Mr. Grogan typed the telegram. It was addressed to Mrs. Rosa Sandoval, 1129 G Street, Ithaca, California, and in the telegram the War Department informed Mrs. Sandoval that her son, Juan Domingo Sandoval, had been killed in action.

Mr. Grogan handed the message to Homer. He then took a long drink from the bottle he kept in the drawer beside his chair. Homer folded the telegram, put it in an envelope, sealed the envelope, put the envelope in his cap and left the office. When the messenger was gone, the old telegraph operator lifted his voice, also singing *Rock of Ages*. For once upon a time he too had been as young as any man.

4. At Home

MUSIC CAME from the Macauley house on Santa Clara Avenue. Bess and Mrs. Macauley played *All the World Will Be Jealous of Me*. They played the song for the soldier Marcus, wherever he happened to be, because it was the song he loved best. Mary Arena came into the parlor from the house next door, and stood beside Bess at the piano and soon began to sing. She sang for Marcus, who was all the world to *her*. The small boy Ulysses listened and watched. Something about everything was mysterious, and he wanted to find out what it was, even though he was half asleep. At last he summoned up enough energy to say:

"Where's Marcus?"

"Marcus is in the Army," Mrs. Macauley said.

"When is he coming home?"

"When the War is over."

"Tomorrow?"

"No, not tomorrow."

"When?"

"We don't know. We're waiting."

"Then where is my father?" Ulysses said. "If we wait, will *he* come home like Marcus, too?"

"No, not that way. He won't come walking down the street, up the steps, across the porch, and on into the house, as he used to do."

This was too much for the boy, and as there was only one word by which to hope for something like truth and comfort, he said this word:

"Why?"

"Two years ago your father died, Ulysses. But as long as we are alive, as long as we are together, as long as *two* of us are left, and remember him, nothing in the world can take him from us."

The boy thought about this a moment and then remembered what he had witnessed earlier that day.

"What are the gophers?" he said.

His mother was not unprepared for such a question. She knew that he had eyes, and beyond eyes vision, and beyond vision heart and love and hunger—to know.

"They share this earth with us. They have life, just as we do. They are part of us, and part of all things that live."

"Then, where is Homer?" he said.

"Yesterday your brother found himself a job after school. He will be home at midnight, when you're fast asleep."

Ulysses tried hard to stay awake, but it was no longer possible.

Mrs. Macauley looked from the boy to his sister Bess. "Put him to bed," she said.

Bess and Mary took the boy to his room. When they were gone and Mrs. Macauley sat alone, she thought she heard a footstep and turned. There at the door she thought she saw Matthew Macauley, as if he were Ulysses himself all over again instead of a grown man who had died so recently and yet so long ago.

5. Mrs. Sandoval

THE MESSENGER got off his bicycle in front of the house of Mrs. Rosa Sandoval. He went to the door and knocked gently. He knew almost immediately that someone was inside the house. He could not hear anything, but he was sure the knock was bringing someone to the door and he was most eager to see who this person would be—this woman named Rosa Sandoval. The door was not a long time opening, but there was no hurry in the way it moved on its hinges. The movement of the door was as if, whoever she was, she had nothing in the world to fear. Then the door was open, and there she was.

To Homer the Mexican woman was beautiful. He could see that she had been patient all her life, so that now, after years of it, her lips were set in a gentle smile. But like all people who never receive telegrams the appearance of a messenger at the front door is full of terrible implications. Homer knew that Mrs. Rosa Sandoval was shocked to see him. Her first word was the first word of all surprise. She said "Oh," as if instead of a messenger she had thought of opening the door to someone she had known a long time and would be pleased to sit down with. She studied Homer's eyes and Homer knew that she knew the message was not a welcome one.

It wasn't Homer's fault. His work was to deliver telegrams. Even so, he felt awkward and almost as if he *alone* were responsible for what had happened. At the same time he wanted to come right out and say, "I'm only a messenger, Mrs. Sandoval. I'm very sorry I must bring you a telegram like this, but it is only because it is my work to do so."

"Mrs. Rosa Sandoval, 1129 G Street?" Homer said. He extended the telegram to the Mexican woman, but she would not touch it.

"Are you Mrs. Sandoval?"

"Please. Please come in." She paused for a moment and looked at the boy standing awkwardly as near the door as he could be and still be inside the house.

"Please," she said, "what does the telegram say?"

"Mrs. Sandoval," the messenger said, "the telegram says—"

But now the woman interrupted him. "But you must *open* the telegram and *read* it to me," she said. "You have not opened it."

"Yes, ma'am," Homer said as if he were speaking to a school teacher who had just corrected him.

He opened the telegram with nervous fingers. The Mexican woman stooped to pick up the torn envelope. As she did so she said, "Who sent the telegram—my son Juan Domingo?"

"No, ma'am. The telegram is from the War Department."

"War Department?" the Mexican woman said.

"Mrs. Sandoval," Homer said swiftly, "your son is dead. Maybe it's a mistake. Maybe it wasn't your son. Maybe it was somebody else. The telegram *says* it was Juan Domingo. But maybe the telegram is wrong."

The Mexican woman pretended not to hear.

"Oh, do not be afraid," she said. "Come inside. I will bring you candy." She took the boy's arm and brought him to the table at the center of the room and there she made him sit.

"All boys like candy," she said. She went into another room and soon returned with an old chocolate candy box. She opened the box at the table and in it Homer saw a strange kind of candy.

"Here," she said, "Eat this candy. All boys like candy."

Homer took a piece of the candy from the box, put it into his mouth and tried to chew.

"You would not bring me a bad telegram," she said.

Homer sat chewing the dry candy while the Mexican woman talked. "It is our own candy," she said, "from cactus."

Now, suddenly she began to make strange soft breathing sounds, holding herself in, as if weeping were a disgrace. Homer wanted to get up and run but he knew he would stay. He even thought he might stay the rest of his life. He just didn't know what else to do to try to make the woman less unhappy, and if she had *asked* him to take the place of her son, he would not have been able to refuse, because he would not have known how. He got to his feet as if by standing he meant to begin correcting what could not be corrected and then he knew the foolishness of this intention and became more awkward than ever. In his heart he was saying over and over again, "What can I do? What the hell can *I* do? I'm only the messenger."

The woman suddenly took him in her arms, saying, "My little boy, my little boy!"

He didn't know why, because he only felt wounded by the whole thing, but for some reason he felt sick and thought he would need to vomit. He didn't *dislike* the woman, but what was happening to her seemed so wrong and so unnecessary that he didn't know if he ever wanted to go on living again, even.

"Come now," the woman said. "Sit down here." She forced him into another chair and stood over him. "Let me look at you." She looked at him strangely and, sick everywhere within himself, the messenger could not move. He felt neither love nor hate but something very close to disgust, but at the same time he felt great compassion, not for the poor woman alone, but for all things and the terrible way of their enduring and dying. He saw her back in time, a beautiful young woman sitting beside the crib of her infant son. He saw her looking down at this amazing human thing, speechless and helpless and full of the world to come. He saw her rocking the crib and he heard her singing to the child. Now look at her, he said to himself.

He was on his bicycle suddenly, riding swiftly down the dark street, tears coming out of his eyes, his mouth whispering crazy young curses. When he got back to the telegraph office the tears had stopped, but everything else had started and he knew there would be no stopping them. "Otherwise I'm just as good as dead myself," he said, as if someone were listening whose hearing was not very good.

6. Mr. Grogan

HOMER SAT across the table from Mr. Grogan. The telegraph wires were silent now, but suddenly the box began to rattle. Homer waited for Mr. Grogan to answer the call, but Mr. Grogan did not answer it. Homer ran around the table.

"Mr. Grogan," he said, "they're calling you!" He shook the man gently.

"Mr. Grogan, wake up! Wake up!"

Homer ran to the water jar and filled a paper cup full of water. He ran back to the old telegraph operator, but he was afraid to follow the instructions he had been given. He put the cup down on the table and shook Mr. Grogan again.

"Mr. Grogan, wake up! They're calling you!"

Homer splashed the cup of water into the telegraph operator's face. Mr. Grogan sat up with a start, opened his eyes, looked at Homer, listened to the telegraph box, and then answered the call.

"That's right, my boy. Now, quick! A cup of black coffee. Hurry!"

Homer ran out of the office to Corbett's. When he got back, the old telegraph operator's eyes were almost closed again, but he was still doing his work.

"That's right, boy," he said. "Don't worry. Don't be afraid. That's exactly right."

Mr. Grogan stopped the telegrapher at the other end of the wire a moment and began to sip the coffee. "First splash the cold water, then fetch the black coffee."

"Yes, sir," Homer said. "Is it an important telegram?"

"No," Mr. Grogan said. "It is most *unimportant*. Business. The accumulating of money. It's a night letter. You won't have to deliver it tonight. Most unimportant. But very important for me to receive it."

He lifted his voice now because he was awake and strong again. "They've been wanting to retire me for years. They've been wanting to put in the machines they're inventing all over the place—Multiplexes and Teletypes. Machines instead of human beings!" He spoke softly now, as if to himself or to the people who were seeking to put him out of his place in the world. "I wouldn't know what to do with myself if I didn't have this job. I guess I'd die in a week. I've worked all my life and I'm not going to stop now."

"Yes, sir," Homer said.

"I know I can count on you to help me, my boy." He rattled the bug. The answer came and he began to type the telegram, but as he typed he spoke with a kind of pride and vigor which pleased Homer very much. "Trying to put me out of my job! Why, I was the fastest telegrapher in the world. Faster than Wolinsky, even, sending and receiving

both—and no mistakes. Willie Grogan. Telegraph opera-
tors all over the world know that name. They know Willie
Grogan was the best of them all!" He paused now and
smiled at the messenger—the boy from the slums who
had come to work last night, just in time.

"Sing another song, my boy."

Without thinking, Homer began to sing the old hymn,
Amazing Grace.

7. Mrs. Macauley

MRS. MACAULAY SAT in the old rocking chair in the parlor
of the house on Santa Clara Avenue waiting for her son to
come home. He reached the parlor a little after midnight.
He was grimy and tired and sleepy, but at the same time
she could see that he was startled and restless. She knew
that when he spoke his voice would be hushed, as the voice
of her husband, this boy's father, had been. He stood a
long time in the dark room, just being there. And then, instead of beginning with the things most important to talk
about, he said, "Everything's all right. I don't want you to

sit up this way *every* night." He paused and had to say
again, "Everything's all right."

"I know," his mother said. "Now sit down."

He moved to sit in the old overstuffed chair but instead
he collapsed. His mother smiled.

"Well," she said. "I know you're tired, but I can see
you're troubled, too. What is it?"

The boy waited a moment and then began to speak very
swiftly, but very quietly, too. "I had to deliver a telegram
to a lady over on G Street," he said. "She was a Mexican
lady." He stopped suddenly and got to his feet.

"I don't know how to tell you about this," he said, "because—well, the telegram was from the War Department.
Her son was killed, but she wouldn't believe it. She just
wouldn't believe it. I never saw anybody hurt that way before. She made me eat candy—made out of cactus.
She hugged me and said *I* was her boy. I didn't care about
that if it helped her. I didn't even care about the candy."
He stopped again. "She kept looking at me as if *I* were her
boy and for a while I wasn't sure I wasn't, I felt so bad.
When I got back to the office the old telegraph operator,
Mr. Grogan—he was drunk, just as he said he would be. I
did what he *told* me to do—splashed water in his face and
got him a cup of black coffee to keep him awake. If he
doesn't do his work they'll put him on a pension, and he
doesn't want that. I got him sober all right and he did his
work all right and then he told me about himself, and then
we sang."

He stopped talking to walk about the room a moment.
He went on, standing at the open door and looking away
from his mother. "All of a sudden," he said, "I feel
different—not like I ever felt before. Even when Papa died
I didn't feel *this* way. In two days everything is changed.
I'm lonely and I don't know what I'm lonely *for*."

His mother didn't speak, waiting for him to go on. "I
don't know what's happening, or why it's happening but
no matter what happens, don't let anything hurt *you* that
way."

The woman waited to see if he had anything more to
say, and as he didn't she began to speak. "Everything *is*

changed," she said—"for you. But it is still the same, too. The loneliness you feel has come to you because you are no longer a child. But the world has always been full of that loneliness. If a message comes to me as to the Mexican woman tonight, I can't tell you what I shall do. I don't know." She stopped suddenly, and then after a moment went on, almost cheerfully. "What did you have for supper?"

"Pie," Homer said—"apple, and cocoanut cream. The manager of the office paid for them. He's the greatest guy I ever met."

"I'll send Bess with a lunch tomorrow."

"I don't want any lunch. We like to go out and buy something and sit down and eat together. You don't have to go to the trouble of making a lunch." He stopped. "This job is the greatest thing that ever happened to me, but it sure makes school seem silly."

"Of course," Mrs. Macauley said. "Schools are only to keep children off the streets, but sooner or later they've got to go out into the streets, whether they like it or not. It's natural for fathers and mothers to be afraid of the world for their children but there's nothing for them to be afraid of. The world is full of frightened little children. Being frightened, they frighten each other. Try to understand," she went on. "Try to love everyone you meet. I shall be in this parlor waiting for you every night. But you needn't come in and talk to me unless you wish to do so. I shall understand. I know there shall be times when your heart shall be unable to give your tongue one word of speech to utter." She stopped now and looked at the boy.

"You're tired, so go along to sleep, now," Mrs. Macauley said.

"O.K.," the boy said, and went to his room.

8. Bess and Mary

AT SEVEN in the morning the alarm clock clicked—that's all—and Homer Macauley sat up. He adjusted the clock so that the alarm would not go off. He then got out of bed and brought out his body-building course from New York and began reading the instructions for the day. His brother Ulysses watched, as he always did, awakening with Homer at the click just before the alarm, which Homer never allowed to go off. The body-building course from New York consisted of a printed booklet and an elastic stretcher. Homer turned to Lesson 7 while Ulysses crowded in under his arm to be nearer the mysterious stuff. After some ordinary preliminary exercises, including deep breathing, Homer lay flat on his back and lifted his legs stiffly from the floor.

"What's that?" Ulysses said.

"Exercises.

"What for?"

"Muscle."

"Going to be the strongest man in the world?"

"Naah."

"What, then?"

"You go back to sleep," Homer said.

Ulysses got back in bed but sat up, watching. At last Homer began to get dressed.

"Where you going?"

"School."

"Going to learn something?"

"Yes, and I'm going to run the two-twenty low hurdles, too."

"Where you going to run 'em?"

"I'm not going to run 'em anywhere. They're wood frames every ten or fifteen yards that you've got to jump over as you run."

"Why?"

"Well, it's a race. Everybody born in this town runs the two-twenty low hurdles. It's the big race of Ithaca. The manager of the telegraph office where I work ran the two-twenty low hurdles when *he* went to Ithaca High. He was Valley Champion."

"What's Valley Champion?"

"That's the best."

"You going to be the best?"

"I'm going to *try*. Now go back to sleep."

Ulysses slipped down in bed, but as he did so he said, "Tomorrow—" then corrected himself—"*Yesterday* I saw the train."

Homer knew what his brother was telling him. He remembered his own fascination with the passing of a train. "How was it?"

"There was a black man, waved."

"Did you wave back?"

"First I waved first. Then he waved first. Then I waved. Then he waved. He said, 'Going home!' " Ulysses looked at his brother. "When are *we* going home?"

"We're home *now*."

"Then why didn't he come here?"

"Everybody's got a different home. Some East, some West, some North, some South. We're West."

"Is West the best?"

"I don't know. I haven't been anywhere else."

"Are you going?"

"Some day."

"Where?"

"New York."

"Where's New York?"

"East. After New York, London. After London, Paris. After Paris, Berlin. Then Vienna, Rome, Moscow, Stockholm some day I'm going to all the great cities of the world."

"Going to come back?"

"Sure."

"Going to be glad?"

"Sure."

"Why?"

"It's always good to get back, that's why."

The little brother pleaded earnestly. "Don't go."

"I'm not going *now*. I'm going to school now, that's all."

"Don't *ever* go," Ulysses said.

"It's going to be a long time before I go. So you go back to sleep."

"All right," Ulysses said. "Going to run the twenty-two?"

"The *two-twenty*."

When Homer sat down at the breakfast table his sister Bess was waiting for him. He bowed his head a moment, lifted it, and began to eat.

"What prayer did you say?" Bess said.

"The one I *always* say at the table," Homer said, and then quoted it, saying the words exactly as he had learned to say them when he had scarcely known how to speak.

"Be present at our table, Lord.
Be here and everywhere adored.
These creatures bless, and grant that we
May feast in Paradise with Thee.
Amen."

"Oh, that's old. Besides, you don't even know what you're saying."

"I know all right. What prayer did *you* say?"

"Tell me first what the words mean."

"They mean what they *say*."

"Well, what *do* they say?"

"Be present at our table, Lord," Homer said. "That means—Be present at our table, Lord. Be here and everywhere adored—that means let good things be respected here and everywhere else. These creatures—that means us, and everybody else. Bless means to watch over, or something like that. And grant that we may feast in Paradise with Thee. Well, that means *exactly* what it says, or nothing. Take your choice. Just grant that we may feast in Paradise with Thee, that's all. I'm going to run the two-twenty low hurdles at the track meet today. It's an important race. Mr. Spangler ran it when *he* went to Ithaca High. You've got to run and jump *both* in that race. He carries a hard-boiled egg around with him for luck."

"Carrying a hard-boiled egg around for luck is superstition," Bess said.

"Who cares about that. He sent me for two day-old pies from Chatterton's—apple, and cocoanut cream. Two for a quarter. Fresh pies are a quarter each, so if you've only got a quarter to spend, you get only one. Day-old pies are *two* for a quarter, so you get two. Half of each pie for me and half for Mr. Grogan—but he can only eat one or two slices altogether. That gives me a lot of pie to eat. Mr. Grogan likes to drink more than eat."

Mary Arena, the neighbor girl, came into the kitchen by way of the back door. She brought with her a small Woolworth bowl and put it on the table. Homer got up.

"Here, Mary. Sit down."

"Oh, no, Homer. You go ahead with your breakfast. Try the stewed dried peaches that I made for my father."

"O.K.," Homer said. "How is your father?"

"Just fine. First thing this morning when he came to the table he said, 'Any letters? Any new letters from Marcus?' "

"We'll be getting another letter soon," Bess said. She got up from the table. "Come on, Mary. Let's go."

"To tell you the truth," Mary said to Mrs. Macauley, "I'm getting sick and tired of going to college. It's just like high school. I'm too old to be going to school. Times have changed. I'd really like to go out and find myself a job somewhere."

"And so would I," Bess said.

"Nonsense," Mrs. Macauley said. "You're both children — Seventeen years old. Your father has a good job, Mary, and your *brother*, Bess."

"But it just doesn't seem right," Mary said. "Marcus in the Army, and the whole world gouging each other's eyes out."

Homer watched the girls go. "What about *that?*" he said.

"Why, it's perfectly natural for a couple of girls to want to get out and flap their wings," Mrs. Macauley said.

"I don't mean a couple of girls wanting to get out and flap their wings. I mean Mary."

"Mary's a sweet, unaffected, childlike girl. She's the most childlike girl I've ever known, and I'm glad Marcus is in love with her."

"Ma," Homer said impatiently, "I know all about *that.* That isn't what I'm talking about." He paused and said, "Oh, well, I got to get going."

Mrs. Macauley watched him go, and then suddenly out of the corner of her eye she saw Ulysses in his nightshirt. He looked up at her, precisely as any small animal looks up at the female of its kind which is its own. The expression of his face was deeply serious and incredibly charming. "Why does he say, 'Weep no more?' "

"Who?"

"The black man on the train."

"It's a song." She took his hand. "Come on, now, put on your clothes."

"Will he be on the train again today?"

Mrs. Macauley thought a moment. "Yes," she said.

9. The Veteran

ON HIS WAY to school Homer Macauley passed a picket
fence protecting an empty lot full of weeds on San Beni-
to Avenue. The fence was old and rotten and had no use
other than to ornament a small area of waste, and to
protect a group of weed tribes which surely needed
no protection. The daytime school student and nighttime
telegraph messenger brought his bicycle to a dynamic skid-
ding halt, dropped the contraption and hurried to the fence
as if there he would discover something extremely fleeting
and apt to be lost if he didn't hurry. The fence was about a

foot higher than the regulation low hurdles. Homer studied
the fence, the area beyond it, the running area before it,
and then measured the height of the fence, which was con-
siderably above his waist. He went back ten yards, and
then without any announcement from himself to himself he
turned in a fury and ran toward the fence. When he was
near enough he made a beautiful hurdle, kicked the fence,
knocked down part of it, and himself fell in the weeds, but
got right up and went back for another try. Altogether
Homer made seven tries, not one of which was successful.
He stopped only when the whole fence had been brought
down into still greater ruin.

An old man with a walking stick came out of the house
across the street, smoking a pipe, and quietly watched
Homer. Just as Homer was getting up from the last spill
and was brushing himself off, the man spoke.

"What you doing?"

"Hurdling."

"Hurt yourself?"

"Naaah, the fence is a little too high, that's all. The weeds
are slippery too."

The old man looked at the weeds a moment and then
said, "Those are milkweeds. They make good feed for
rabbits. Rabbits like them. I used to have a hutch of
rabbits about eleven years ago, but somebody opened the
door in the middle of the night and they ran away."

"What did he open the door for?"

"Well, I don't know. I never did find out who did it. I
lost thirty-three head of the prettiest rabbits you ever saw.
Pink-eyes, cat-faces, Belgians, and two or three other kinds
—never did find out."

"Do you like rabbits?" Homer said.

"They're gentle little animals. Domestic rabbits are
very mild-mannered." The old man looked around among
the weeds of the empty lot. "Thirty-three rabbits out in the
open for eleven years. There's no telling how many of
them there are now—not the way *they* breed. I wouldn't be
surprised if this whole city is full of wild rabbits now."

"*I* never see any of them."

"Maybe not. But they're here—somewhere. The whole

city's overrun with them, most likely. A couple more years and they'll be a serious problem."

Even so, Homer got on his bike. "Well, I got to go now."

"Come again," the old man said. "Any time at all. You're welcome."

"Thanks," Homer said. "I'm going to run the two-twenty low hurdles at the high school track meet this afternoon."

"Didn't go to high school, myself, but I fought in the Spanish-American War."

"Yes, sir. Well, so long!"

"Oh, yes," the old man said, but he was talking to himself now. "Ran like a rabbit half the time."

Homer disappeared around the corner, and the old man strolled back to his little broken-down house, puffing his pipe and looking around.

10. The Ancient History Class

ON THE TRACK of the athletic field at Ithaca High School the hurdles were set for the 220-yard low hurdle race. Now, in the morning, four boys were running a practice race. Each ran well, under control, and each hurdled with good form. Coach Byfield, stop-watch in hand, came up to the winner.

"That was better, Ackley," he said to a boy who was surely not common, but for all that surely not terribly *uncommon*, either. He was a boy who had the resigned manner of one whose family had not in recent decades been in want of food, clothing or shelter, who on occasion entertained others of similar good fortune.

"You've got a lot to learn yet," the coach said to the boy, "but I think you'll be able to win the race this afternoon."

"I'll try my best, sir."

"You won't be having any real competition today, but you'll have plenty in two weeks at the Valley Meet. Go to the shower now and take it easy until this afternoon."

"Yes, sir," the boy said.

The other three runners were over to one side, watching and listening.

"He may *act* like a sissy," one of the boys said, "but he always comes in first. What's the matter with you, Sam?"

"What's the matter with *me?*" Sam said. "What's the matter with *you?* Why don't *you* beat him?"

"I came in second."

"Second's no better than third," the third boy said.

"Hubert Ackley the Third, beating us!" Sam said. "We ought to be ashamed of ourselves."

"Sure," the second boy said, "but we've got no alibis. He just runs a better race, that's all."

The coach turned to these three and, in an altogether different tone of voice, said, "O.K., you guys. You're not so good you can stand around and be proud of yourselves. Get to your marks and give it another try."

Without a word the boys went to their marks and the coach sent them off for another run of the race. After they began to run, he decided he'd run them a couple of more times before the afternoon meet. He seemed determined to have Hubert Ackley III win the race.

The ancient history classroom was swiftly filling, as the teacher, old Miss Hicks, waited for the final bell and the kind of order and quiet which in her class was the sign for the beginning of another stab at the business of trying to educate, if not entertain, the boys and girls of Ithaca, now at high school and soon, at least theoretically, to be ready for the world. Homer Macauley watched a girl named Helen Eliot walk from the door to her desk. Without a doubt

this girl was the most beautiful girl in the world. Besides
that, she was a snob—which Homer refused to believe.
Following her came Hubert Ackley III. When Hubert
reached Helen the two whispered a moment, which made
Homer sick with envy and anger. The final bell rang, and
Miss Hicks said, "All right. Silence, please. Who's absent?"

"I am," a boy said. His name was Joe Terranova, and he
was the low comedian of the class. The four or five of Joe's
faithful, the members of his religious cult of comedy, his
disciples, were instant in their response and appreciation of
his swift and goofy wit. But Helen Eliot and Hubert Ackley turned and frowned at these Holy Rollers of the classroom, these bad-mannered offspring of slum-dwellers. This
in turn annoyed Homer so much that when everyone else
had stopped laughing he burst out with an artificial Hah
Hah Hah, which he sent almost directly into the faces of
Hubert, whom he despised, and Helen, whom he adored.
Then he turned swiftly to Joe and said, "As for you, Joe,
shut up when Miss Hicks is talking."

"None of your nonsense now, Joseph Terranova," Miss
Hicks said. And turning to Homer, "Or yours, Homer Macauley." She paused a moment to look the class over. "We
will take up the Assyrians where we left off yesterday. I
want everyone's undivided attention—everyone's *contin-
uous* undivided attention. First we will read from our ancient history textbook. Then we will have an oral discussion of what we have read."

The low comedian could not resist this opportunity for
horseplay. "No, Miss Hicks," he suggested. "Let's not discuss it orally. Let's discuss it silently, so I can sleep." Again
the faithful roared with laughter and the snobs turned
away, disgusted. Miss Hicks did not answer the comedian
immediately. It was difficult not to enjoy his wit, and she
didn't want it to stop, but at the same time it was absolutely necessary to keep him in line. At last she spoke.

"You must not be unkind, especially when it happens
that you're right."

"Well, I'm sorry, Miss Hicks. I guess I just can't help it.
Oral discussion! What other kind of discussion is there?
But O.K., I'm sorry." Now, with a kind of spoofing of

himself and of his own presumptuousness, he waved to her, saying patronizingly, "Go ahead, Miss Hicks."

"Thank you," the teacher said. "Now, everybody—wide awake!"

"Wide awake?" Joe said. "Look at them—they're all fast asleep with their eyes wide open."

"Another interruption," the teacher said, "and I'll have to ask you to go to the principal's office."

"I'm only trying to get myself a little education," Joe said.

"Ah, shut up," Homer said to his friend. "You don't have to show off all the time, Joe. Everybody knows how smart you are."

"Not another word," Miss Hicks said. "Not another word from either of you. Page 117, paragraph two." Everyone turned to the page and found the place. "Ancient history," the teacher continued, "may *seem* to be a dull and unnecessary study. At a time like the present, when so much history is going on in our own world, the history of another world—long since ended—may seem useless to study and understand. Such a notion, however, is incorrect. It is very important for us to know of other times, other cultures, other peoples, and other worlds. Who'll volunteer to come to the head of the class and read?" Two girls and Hubert Ackley III raised their hands.

Joe, the comedian, glanced at Homer, and said, "Get a load of that guy, will you?"

Of the two girls who had volunteered the teacher chose Helen Eliot. Homer watched her walk to the front of the class. She just stood there, being very beautiful, and then in the purest and most liquid voice imaginable she began to read, while Homer marveled at the incredible miracle of such a person and such a voice.

"The Assyrians," Helen read, "long of nose, hair and beard, developed Nineveh in the north to a position of great power. After many vicissitudes with the Hittites, Egyptians and others, they conquered Babylon under the reign of Tiglath Pileser the First, in eleven hundred B.C. For centuries afterward, the power veered between Nineveh built of stone and Babylon built of brick. There is no

connection between the names 'Syrian' and 'Assyrian,' and
the Assyrians were to fight the Syrians until Tiglath Pileser
the Third conquered them and exiled the ten lost tribes of
Israel."

Helen paused for a fresh supply of breath with which to
read the next paragraph, but before she could begin to read
again, Homer Macauley said, "How about Hubert *Ackley*
the Third? Who did *he* conquer, or what did he do?"

The well-bred boy got to his feet in a kind of decent bit-
terness. "Miss Hicks," he said very earnestly, "I cannot allow such malicious mischief to go uncorrected or un-
punished. I must ask you to order Mr. Macauley to go to
the principal's office—or," he said very deliberately, "I
shall have to take the matter into my own hands."

Homer jumped out of his seat. "Ah, shut up! Your name
is Hubert Ackley the Third, isn't it? Well, what did you
ever do, or for that matter what did Hubert Ackley the
Second ever do, or what did Hubert Ackley the First ever
do?" He paused a moment and then faced Miss Hicks
and Helen Eliot. "I think that's a good intelligent question." Then he turned to Hubert Ackley and repeated the
question. "What did they do?"

"Well," Hubert said, "at least no Ackley has ever been a
common—" He stopped to seek an appropriately withering
word, and then said, "—fanfaron," a word nobody else in
Ithaca had ever before heard.

"Fanfaron?" Homer said. "What's that mean, Miss
Hicks?" As she was not ready with a definition of the
word, Homer turned quickly to Hubert Ackley and went
on, "Listen, number three, don't be calling me something I
never even *heard* before."

"A fanfaron," Hubert said, "is a hoodlum—a braggart."
And he stopped to find another, *lower* word.

"Ah, shut up," Homer said.

He glanced at Helen Eliot and smiled the famous Macauley smile. *"Fanfaron!"* he repeated. "What kind of
cussing is that?" Then he sat down.

Helen Elliot waited for a sign from the teacher to go on
reading. Miss Hicks, however, did not give the sign. Final-

ly Homer understood. He got to his feet and said to Hubert Ackley III, "All right, I apologize. I'm sorry."

"Thank you," the well-bred boy said, and sat down.

The ancient-history teacher looked about the room a moment and then said, "Homer Macauley and Hubert Ackley will remain in their seats after school."

"But, Miss Hicks," Homer said, "what about the track meet?"

"The development of your minds is as important as the development of your bodies. Perhaps more important."

"Miss Hicks," Hubert Ackley said, "I'm afraid Coach Byfield will *insist* on my taking part in the track meet."

"I don't know about Coach Byfield *insisting*," Homer said, "But *I'm* going to run the two-twenty low hurdles, that's all."

Hubert Ackley looked at Homer. "I had no idea you had gone out for that race."

"Well, I have. Miss Hicks, If you let us go this time, I promise never again to make any trouble or to be disobedient or *anything*. And so does Hubert. Don't you?"

"Yes, I do, Miss Hicks," Hubert said.

"You will both stay in after school. Helen, please continue to read."

"The allied armies," Helen read, "of the Chaldeans from the south and the Medes and Persians from the north overcame the Assyrian empire and Nineveh bowed to their might. Nebuchadnezzar the Second ruled over the second Babylonian empire. Then came the great Cyrus, King of Persia, with his hordes of invaders. His conquest, however, was only one of a cycle, for the descendants of this army would later be subjugated by Alexander the Great."

Homer, disgusted now, tired from the work of the night before and lulled by the sweet voice of the girl he believed was made only for himself, slowly dropped his head on his folded arms and began to enjoy something almost the equivalent of sleep. Still he could hear the girl reading.

"From this melting pot," she read, "the world has a heritage of great value. The Mosaic code of the Bible owes some of its principles to some of the laws formulated by Hammurabi, who was called the law-giver. From their system of arithmetic, in which they used the multiple of twelve as well as our familiar ten, we derive our sixty minutes to the hour and 360 degrees to the circle. Arabia gave us our numerals, which are still called Arabic to distinguish them from the Roman system of notation. The Assyrians invented the sundial. The modern apothecary symbols and the signs of the Zodiac originated with the Babylonians. Comparatively recent excavations in Asia Minor have revealed that there was a magnificent empire there."

"A magnificent empire?" Homer dreamed. "Where? In Ithaca in California? Away out to hell and gone? Without any great people, without any great discoveries, without sundials, without numerals, without Zodiacs, without humor, without anything? Where was this great empire?" He decided to sit up and look around again. He saw only the face of Helen Eliot, perhaps the greatest empire of them all, and he heard her liquid voice, perhaps the greatest achievement of pathetic mankind.

"The Hittites," she said, "had swung down the coast and over into Egypt. They mingled their blood with the Hebrew tribes and gave to the Hebrews the Hittite nose."

Helen stopped reading and turned to the ancient-history teacher. "That's the end of the chapter, Miss Hicks."

"Very well, Helen. Thank you for an excellent reading. You may be seated."

11. The Human Nose

MISS HICKS WAITED for Helen to take her seat and then looked over the faces of her pupils. "Now," she said, "what have we learned?"

"That people all over the world have noses," Homer said.

Miss Hicks was not upset by this reply and took it for what it was worth. "What else?"

"That noses," Homer said, "are not only for blowing or to have colds in but also to keep the record of ancient history straight."

Miss Hicks turned away from Homer and said, "Someone else, please. Homer seems to have been carried away by the noses."

"Well, it's in the book, isn't it? What do *they* mention it for? It must be important."

"Perhaps you'd like to make an extemporaneous speech on the nose, Mr. Macauley."

"Well," Homer said, "maybe not exactly a speech—but ancient history tells us one thing." Slowly now, and with a kind of unnecessary emphasis, he continued, "People have always had noses. To prove it all you have to do is look around at everybody in this classroom." He looked around at everybody. "Noses, all over the place." He stopped a moment to decide what else would be possible to say on this theme. "The nose has always been a source of embarrassment to the human race, and the Hittites probably beat up on everybody else because their noses were so big and crooked. It doesn't matter who invented the sundial because sooner or later somebody invents a watch. The important thing is, Who's got the noses?"

Joe the comedian listened with profound interest and admiration, if not envy. Homer continued.

"Some people talk through their noses. A great many people snore through their noses, and a handful of people whistle or sing through them. Some people are led around by their noses, others use the nose for prying and poking into miscellaneous places. Noses have been bitten by mad dogs and movie actors in passionate love scenes. Doors have been slammed on them and they have been caught in eggbeaters and automatic record changers. The nose is stationary, like a tree, but being on a movable object—the head—it suffers great punishment by being taken to places where it is only in the way. The purpose of the nose is to smell what's in the air, but some people sniff with the nose at other people's ideas, manners, or appearances." He looked at Hubert Ackley III and then at Helen Eliot, whose nose, instead of moving upward, for some reason went slightly downward. "These people generally hold their noses toward heaven, as if that were the way to get in. Most animals have nostrils but few have noses, as we understand noses, yet the sense of smell in animals is more highly developed than in man—who has a nose, and no fooling." Homer Macauley took a deep breath and decided to conclude his speech. "The most important thing to remember about the nose—is that it makes trouble, causes wars, breaks up old friendships, and wrecks many happy homes. *Now* can I go to the track meet, Miss Hicks?"

The ancient-history teacher, although pleased by this imaginative discourse on a trivial theme, would not allow its success to interfere with the need for her to maintain order in the classroom. "You will stay in after school, Mr. Macauley, and so will *you*, Mr. Ackley. Now that we have disposed of the matter of noses, someone else please comment on what we have read."

There were no comments.

"Come now," Miss Hicks said. "Somebody else comment—*anybody*."

Joe the comedian answered the call. "Noses are red, violets are blue. Ithaca's dead. California, I love you."

"Anyone else?"

"Big noses are generally on navigators and explorers," a girl said.

"Very good. Henry?"

"I don't know anything about noses," Henry said.

"All right," Joe said, "who is Moses?"

"Moses is in the Bible," Henry said.

"Did he have a nose?"

"Sure he had a nose."

"All right, then. Why don't you say, 'Moses had a nose as big as most noses'?"

"Why should I?"

"To learn a little ancient history, that's why."

"Anybody else?"

Nobody volunteered, so Joe said, "Well, I guess it's up to me, as usual. The hand is faster than the eye, but only the nose runs."

"Miss Hicks," Homer said, "you've got to let me run the two-twenty low hurdles."

"I'm not interested in *any* kind of hurdles," Miss Hicks said. "Anybody else?"

But it was too late. The class bell rang. Everyone got up to leave for the track meet except Homer Macauley and Hubert Ackley III.

12. Miss Hicks

THE BOYS' ATHLETIC COACH of Ithaca High stood in the office of the principal—a man whose last name was Ek, a circumstance duly reported by Mr. Robert Ripley in a daily newspaper cartoon entitled "Believe It or Not." Mr. Ek's first name was Oscar, and not worthy of notice.

"Miss Hicks," the principal said to the coach, "is the oldest and best teacher we have ever had at this school. She was *my* teacher when I attended Ithaca High, and she was your teacher, too, Mr. Byfield. I'm afraid I wouldn't care to go over her head about punishing a couple of unruly boys."

"Hubert Ackley the Third is *not* an unruly boy," the coach said. "Homer Macauley—yes. Hubert Ackley—no. He is a perfect little gentleman."

"Well, he comes from a well-to-do family, at any rate. But if Miss Hicks has asked him to stay in after school, then *in* it is. Perhaps he *is* a perfect little gentleman. But Miss Hicks is the teacher of the ancient history class and she has never been known to punish anyone who has not deserved to be punished. Hubert Ackley will have to run the race some other time."

The matter was surely closed now, the principal felt. The coach turned and left the office. He did not go to the athletic field, however. He went to the ancient history classroom instead. There he found Homer and Hubert and Miss Hicks. He bowed to the old teacher and smiled.

"Miss Hicks," he said, "I have spoken to Mr. Ek about this matter." The implication of his remark was that he had been given authorization to come and liberate Hubert Ackley III. Homer Macauley, however, leaped to his feet as if it were *he* who was to be liberated.

"Not *you*," the coach said. "Mr. Ackley."

"What do you mean?" the ancient-history teacher said.

"Mr. Ackley is to get into his track suit immediately and run the two-twenty low hurdles. We're waiting for him."

"Oh yeah?" Homer said. He was overflowing with righteous indignation. "Well what about Mr. *Macauley?*" There was no reply from the coach, who walked out of the room followed by a somewhat troubled and confused young man—Hubert Ackley III.

"Did you see that, Miss Hicks?" Homer said.

The ancient-history teacher was so upset she could barely speak. At last she managed to whisper, "Mr. Byfield is a liar." Homer was amazed to see Miss Hicks so angry. It made him feel that she was just about the best teacher ever.

"I have taught ancient history at Ithaca High for thirty-five years. I have known hundreds of Ithaca boys and girls. I taught your brother Marcus and your sister Bess, and if you have younger brothers or sisters at home I shall some day teach them, too."

"Just a brother, Ulysses. How *was* Marcus in school?"

"Marcus and Bess were both good students—honest and civilized. Yes, *civilized*. The behavior of ancient peoples had made them civilized from birth. Like yourself, Marcus sometimes spoke out of turn, but he was never a liar. That man came here and deliberately lied to me—just as he lied to me time and again when he sat in this classroom as a boy. He has learned nothing except to toady to those he feels are superior. The two-twenty low hurdles! *Low* indeed!" The ancient-history teacher blew her nose and wiped her eyes.

"Don't feel bad, Miss Hicks," Homer said. "I never knew teachers are human beings like everybody else—and *better*, too! I'll stay in, Miss Hicks. You can punish me."

"I didn't keep you in to punish you," the teacher said. "I have always kept in only those who have meant the most to me. I still don't believe I'm mistaken about Hubert Ackley. I was going to send both of you to the field after a moment, anyway. You were not kept in for punishment, but for education. I watch the growth of spirit in the children who come to my class. You apologized to Hubert Ackley. And even though it embarassed him to do so, because your apology made him unworthy, he graciously accepted your apology. I kept you in after school because I wanted to talk to both of you—one of you from a good well-to-do family, the other from a good poor family. Getting along in this world will be even more difficult for him than for you. I wanted you to know one another a little better. It is very important. I wanted to talk to *both* of you."

"I guess I like Hubert," Homer said, "only he seems to think he's better than the other boys."

"I know how you feel, but every man in the world *is* better than someone else. And not as good as someone *else*. Joseph Terranova is brighter than Hubert, but Hubert is just as honest in his own way. In a democratic state every man is the equal of every other man up to the point of exertion, and after that every man is free to exert himself as he chooses. I am eager for my boys and girls to exert them-

selves about behaving with honor. What my children
appear to be on the surface is no matter to me. I am
fooled neither by gracious manners nor by bad manners. I
am interested in what is truly beneath each kind of manners. Whether one of my children is rich or poor, brilliant
or slow, genius or simple-minded, is no matter to me, if
there is humanity in him—if he has a heart—if he loves
truth and honor—if he respects both his inferiors and his
superiors. If the children of my classroom are human, I do
not want them to be alike in their *manner* of being human.
If they are not corrupt, it does not matter to me how they
differ from one another. I want each of my children to be
himself. I don't want you to be like somebody else just to
please me or to make my work easier. I would soon be
weary of a classroom full of perfect little ladies and gentlemen. I want my children to be *people*—each one separate
—each one special—each one a pleasant and exciting vari-
ation of all the others. I wanted Hubert Ackley here to listen to this with you—to understand with you that if at the
present you do not like him and he does not like you, that
is perfectly natural. I wanted him to know that each of
you will begin to be truly human when, in spite of your
natural dislike of one another, you still respect one another. That is what it means to be civilized—that is what we
are to learn from a study of ancient history. I'm glad I've
spoken to you, rather than to anyone else I know. When
you leave this school—long after you have forgotten *me*—
I shall be watching for you in the world." Again Miss
Hicks blew her nose and touched her handkerchief to her
eyes. "Run along to the athletic field, now."

The second son of the Macauley family of Santa Clara
Avenue in Ithaca, California, got up from his desk and
walked out of the room.

On the athletic field Hubert Ackley and the three boys
who had already raced with him that day were taking their
places in the lanes for the two-twenty low hurdle race.
Homer reached the fifth lane just as the man with the pis-
tol lifted his arm to start the race. Homer went to his mark
with the others. He felt good, but very angry, and he believed that nothing in the world would be able to keep him

from winning this race—the wrong kind of shoes, the wrong kind of clothes for running, no practice, or anything else. He would just naturally win the race.

Hubert Ackley, in the lane next to Homer's lane, turned to him and said, "*You* can't run this race—like *that*."

"No?" Homer said. "Wait and see."

Mr. Byfield, sitting in the grandstand, asked himself, "Who's that starting in the outside lane without track clothes?" Then he remembered who it was.

He decided to stop the race so that he could remove the fifth runner, but it was too late. The gun had been fired and the runners were running. Homer and Hubert took the first hurdle a little ahead of the others, each of them clearing nicely. Homer moved a little ahead of Hubert on the second hurdle and kept moving ahead on the third, fourth, fifth, sixth, seventh and eighth hurdles. But close behind was Hubert Ackley.

Homer reached the ninth hurdle precisely when the coach of Ithaca High also reached it, coming in the opposite direction, so that Homer hurdled straight into the outstretched arms of the athletic coach and the man and the boy fell to the ground. Hubert Ackley stopped running and stopped the other runners. "Stay where you are," he shouted. "Let him get up." Homer got to his feet, and the race resumed.

Everyone in the grandstand, even Helen Eliot, was amazed at what had happened. Now, the ancient-history teacher was at the finish line of the race.

"Come on, Homer!" she said. "Come on, Hubert! Hurry, Sam!—George!—Henry!"

At the next to the last hurdle Hubert caught up with Homer. "Sorry," he said.

"Go ahead," Homer said.

Hubert Ackley moved a little ahead of Homer and now there was no longer very far to go. Homer kicked the last hurdle, but he almost caught up with Hubert. The finish of the race was so close no one could tell who had actually won it. Sam, George and Henry came in soon after.

Furious and bitter, and a little shocked by the fall he had taken, the coach of Ithaca High came running toward the group which Miss Hicks had gathered around her.

"Macauley!" he shouted from a distance of fifteen yards.

When he reached the group he stood panting for breath and glaring at Homer Macaualey.

Then he said, "For the remainder of this semester you will take no part in any school athletic activities."

"Yes, sir," Homer said.

"Now go to my office and stay there."

"Your office?" Homer suddenly remembered that he had to be at work at four o'clock. "What time is it?" he said.

Hubert Ackley looked at his wristwatch. "A quarter to four."

"Go to my office!" Byfield shouted.

"But you don't understand, Mr. Byfield," Homer said. "I've got to go somewhere, and I just can't be late."

Joe Terranova came into the group. "Why should he go to your office? He didn't do anything wrong."

The poor coach had already suffered too much. "You keep your dirty little wop mouth shut!" he shouted. Then he pushed the boy, who went sprawling. But even before he touched the ground, Joe shouted: "W-O-P?"

On his feet again, Joe tackled Byfield as if they were in a football game.

Mr. Ek came running, breathless and bewildered.

"Gentlemen!" he said. "Boys, boys!" He dragged Joe Terranova off the athletic coach, who did not get to his feet.

"Mr. Byfield," the principal said, "what is the meaning of this unusual behavior?"

Speechless, Byfield pointed at Miss Hicks.

"Mr. Byfield owes Joe Terranova an apology," she said.

"Is that so? Is that so, Mr. Byfield?" Mr. Ek said.

"Joe's people *are* from Italy, that's quite true, but they are not to be referred to as wops," Miss Hicks said.

Joe Terranova said, "He doesn't need to apologize to me. If he calls me names, I'll bust him in the mouth. If he beats me up, I'll get my brothers."

"Joseph," Miss Hicks said. "You must allow Mr. Byfield to apologize. You must give him the privilege of once again trying to be an American."

"Yes, that's so," the principal said. "This is America, and the only foreigners here are those who forget that this *is* America." He turned to the man who was still sprawled on the ground. "Mr. Byfield," he commanded.

The athletic coach of Ithaca High School got to his feet. To no one in particular he said, "I apologize," and hurried away.

Joe Terranova and Homer Macauley went off together. Joe walked well, but Homer limped. He had hurt his left leg when Byfield had tried to stop him.

Miss Hicks and Mr. Ek turned to the thirty or forty boys and girls who had gathered around. They were of many types and many nationalities.

"All right, now," Miss Hicks said. "Go along home to your families," and as the boys and girls were all a little bewildered, she added, "Brighten up, brighten up—this is nothing."

"Yes," the principal said, "brighten up, every one of you, please."

The children broke up into groups and walked away.

13. Big Chris

WHEN HOMER MACAULAY swung onto his bicycle after the track meet to get to work as soon as possible, a man named Big Chris walked into Covington's Sporting Goods Store on Tulare Street. He was a huge man, tall, lean and hard, with a great blond beard. He had just come down from the hills around Piedra to see about some new grub and shells and traps. Mr. Covington, the founder and proprietor of the store, began immediately to demonstrate to Big Chris the workings of a rather involved new trap that had just been invented by a man out in Friant. The trap

was enormous and complicated. It was made of steel, lem-
onwood, springs and ropes. Its principle seemed to be to
take the animal, swing it up and around, and hold it off its
feet until the trapper arrived.

"This is brand new," Mr. Covington said, "invented by a
man named Safferty out in Friant. He's applied for a patent and so far he's made only two of them, one a model,
which he sent to the patent office, and this one, which he
sent to me, to sell. The trap is for any kind of animal that
walks. Mr. Safferty calls it 'THE LIFT-THEM-OFF-THEIR-
FEET, SWING-THEM-AROUND, AND-HOLD-THEM SAFFERTY
ALL-ANIMAL TRAP.' He's asking twenty dollars for it. Of
course the trap hasn't been tested, but as you can see for
yourself, it is strong and could very likely lift, swing and
hold a full grown bear with no difficulty at all."

Big Chris listened to the proprietor of the sporting goods
store as a child listens, and behind him Ulysses Macauley
listened with the same fascination, ducking in between the
two men for a better view of the trap. Mr. Covington was
under the impression that Ulysses belonged to Big Chris
and Big Chris was under the impression that Ulysses belonged to Mr. Covington, so that between the two of them
they had no reason to account for the small boy's presence.
As for Ulysses himself, he was under the impression that
he belonged wherever there was something interesting to
see.

"The remarkable thing about this trap," Mr. Covington
said, "is that it will not *hurt* the animal, leaving the fur
whole and undamaged. The trap is guaranteed by Mr. Safferty himself for a period of eleven years. This includes all
parts—the pliancy of the wood, the endurance of the
springs, the steel, the ropes, and all the other parts. Mr.
Safferty, although not a trapper himself, believes this is the
most effective and humane trap in the world. A man close
to seventy, he lives quietly in Friant, reading books and inventing things. He has invented, all told, thirty-seven separate and distinct items of practical usefulness." Mr. Covington stopped his work with the trap. "Now," he said, "I believe the trap is set."

Ulysses, crowding in to watch, moved too far: the trap

closed on him gently but swiftly, lifted him off his feet,
turned him around and held him three feet off the floor,
straight out, horizontally, clamped in. No sound came
from the boy, even though he was a little bewildered. Big
Chris, however, did not take the event so lightly.

"Careful there!" he said to Covington. "I don't want
your son to be hurt."

"My son?" Covington said. "I thought he was *your* son.
I never saw the boy before in my life. He came in with
you."

"He did?" Big Chris said. "I didn't notice. Well, now,
hurry! Get him out of the trap—get him out!"

"Yes, sir," Covington said. "Now let me see."

Big Chris was worried and confused. "What's your
name, boy?" he said.

"Ulysses," the boy in the trap said.

"My name is Big Chris. Now you just hold tight there,
Ulysses, and the man here will get you right out and set
you free." Big Chris turned to Mr. Covington. "Well, come
on now," he said, "get the boy back on his feet."

Mr. Covington, however, was just as confused as Big
Chris. "I'm not sure I remember how Mr. Safferty explained *that* part of the trap. He didn't *demonstrate* the
trap, you see, because—well—we didn't have anything to
demonstrate it *on*. Mr. Safferty only *explained* it. I believe
this is supposed to move out—no, it seems to be immova-
ble."

Now, Big Chris and Mr. Covington went to work on the
trap together, Big Chris holding Ulysses so that if the trap
opened suddenly Ulysses wouldn't fall on his face, and the
other man fooling around with the various parts of the trap
to see if anything would give way.

"Well, hurry now," Big Chris said. "Let's not keep the
boy in the air all day. You're not hurt, are you, Ulysses?"

"No, sir," Ulysses said.

"Well, you just hold tight. We'll get you out of this." He
looked sharply at the boy and then said, "What made you
crowd in there?"

"Watching," Ulysses said.

"Yes, it *is* a fascinating sort of contraption, isn't it? Now

the man here will get you right out and I won't let you fall.
How old are you?"

"Four," Ulysses said.

"Four," Big Chris said. "Well, I'm fifty years older than
you. Now the man here will get you right out, won't you?"
And Big Chris looked sharply at Mr. Covington. "What's
your name?" he said.

"Walter Covington. I own this store."

"Well, that's fine. Now, Walter, get the boy out. Move
that piece of wood there. I'm holding him. Don't you worry, Ulysses. What's your *father's* name?"

"Matthew," Ulysses said.

"Well, he's a lucky man to have a boy like you. A fellow
with his eyes open. I'd give the world to have a boy like
you, but I never met the right woman. I met a girl in Okla-
homa thirty years ago but she went off with another fellow.
Have you got it there, Walter?"

"Not yet," Mr. Covington said. "But I'll get it. I believe
this is supposed to—no. Mr. Safferty *explained* how to get
the animal out of the trap, but it seems I just can't get the
hang of it. Maybe the principle changes when it's a small
boy instead of an animal."

Two men, a woman with a small girl, and two boys of
nine or ten came into the store to watch.

"What's the matter?" one of the boys said.

"We've got a boy caught in a trap here," Mr. Covington
said. "A boy named Ulysses."

"How'd he get in?" one of the men said. "Shall I call a
doctor?"

"No, he isn't hurt," Big Chris said. "The boy's all right.
He's just off his feet, that's all."

"Maybe you ought to call the police," the woman said.

"No, lady," Big Chris said. "He's just caught in the trap.
The man here—Walter—he'll get the boy out."

"Well," the lady said, "it's a shame the way little boys
are made to suffer by all sorts of ridiculous mechanical
devices."

"The boy's all right, lady," Big Chris said. "He *isn't*
suffering."

"Well," the lady said, "if he were *my* boy, I'd have the

police on you in two minutes." She went away in a huff, dragging her little daughter along.

"I want to see, I want to see!" the little girl cried. "Everybody gets to see but *me!*" The woman shook the little girl and dragged her out of the store.

"Now, don't you worry, Ulysses," Big Chris said. "We'll get you out of this in no time at all."

Mr. Covington, however, gave up. "Maybe I'd better telephone Mr. Safferty," he said. "*I* can't get the boy out."

"Got to stay here?" Ulysses said.

"No, you don't, boy," Big Chris said. "No, by God, you don't."

A boy with a dozen afternoon papers under his arm came into the store, crowded into the scene, looked at Ulysses, looked at the people, looked at Ulysses again, and then spoke.

"Hello, Ulysses," he said. "What you doing?"

"Hello, Auggie," Ulysses said. "Caught."

"What for?"

"Got caught."

The newsboy tried to help Big Chris, but only got in the way. He looked around, panic-stricken and paralyzed, but after a moment of confusion bolted for the street. He ran straight to the telegraph office. Homer wasn't there, so he ran into the street again, running one way and then the other, bumping into people and shouting the day's headline all at the same time.

A woman who had been bumped said to herself. "Crazy! —from trying to sell papers!"

Auggie ran a full block, got out into the middle of the street to look around in four directions for Homer. As luck would have it, Homer appeared around a corner on his bicycle. Auggie ran toward Homer, shouting at him with all his might.

"Homer! You've got to come right away!"

Homer got off his bicycle. "What's the matter, Auggie?"

"Something's happened!" Auggie shouted, even though Homer was right beside him. "You've got to come with me!" He took Homer by the arm.

"But what's the matter?"

"Over at Covington's. Hurry—you've got to come!"

"Ah," Homer said, "you want to show me some new fishing tackle or a rifle or something in the window. I can't go around looking at things any more, Auggie. I'm working now. I've got to go to work."

Homer got back on his wheel and began to ride away, but Augie took hold of the bike seat and trotted beside him, pushing the bike toward Covington's. "Homer, you've got to come with me! He's caught—he can't get out!"

"What are you talking about?"

Now, they were across the street from Covington's. There was a small crowd in front of the store, and Homer began to be a little frightened. Auggie pointed at the people. The two boys pushed through the crowd into the store, to the trap. There in the trap was Homer's brother Ulysses, and around the trap were Big Chris, Mr. Covington, and a number of strange men and women and boys.

"Ulysses!" Homer shouted.

"Hello, Homer," Ulysses said.

Homer spoke to Mr. Covington. "What's my brother doing in *that* thing?" he said.

"He got caught," Mr. Covington said.

"What are all these people doing here? Go home," he said to the people. "Can't a small boy get caught in a trap without the whole world hanging around?"

"Yes," Mr. Covington said, "I'll have to ask you people to go, who are not customers." Mr. Covington studied the people. "Mr. Wallace," he said, "you can stay. You trade here, and you, Mr. Sickert. George. Mr. Spindle. Shorty."

"*I* trade here," a man said. "I bought fish hooks here not more than a week ago'"

"Yes," Mr. Covington said, "fish hooks. The rest of you will have to go." Only two people moved away a little.

"Don't worry, Ulysses," Homer said. "Everything's going to be all right now. It's a good thing Auggie found me. Auggie, run over to the telegraph office and tell Mr. Spangler my brother Ulysses is caught in a trap at Covington's and I'm trying to get him out. I'm late already but tell him I'll be over as soon as I get Ulysses out of the trap. Hurry now."

Auggie turned and ran. He bumped into a policeman who was coming into the store and almost knocked the man down.

"What's all the commotion about?" the policeman said.

"We've got a small boy caught in a trap here," Mr. Covington said. "Can't get him out."

"Let me look into this," the policeman said. He looked at Ulysses, and then at the people.

"All right now," he said, "get along with you, all of you. These things happen every day. You've got better things to do than stand around and watch a small boy in a trap." The policeman moved the people out of the store and locked the front door. He went to Mr. Covington and Big Chris. "Now, let's get this boy out of this thing and send him home."

"Yes," Mr. Covington said, "and the sooner the better. You've got my shop closed at four-thirty in the afternoon."

"Well, how does this thing work?" Homer said.

"It's a new trap," Mr. Covington said—"just invented by Mr. Wilfred Safferty of Friant. He's asking twenty dollars for it and a patent's been applied for."

"Well, get my brother out of it," Homer said, "or get someone who *can*. Get Mr. Safferty."

"I've already tried to telephone Mr. Safferty, but the telephone is out of order," Mr. Covington said.

"Out of order?" Homer shouted. He was very angry about the whole thing. "What do I care if the phone's out of order? Get the man down here and get my brother out of the trap."

"Yes, I think you'd better do that," the policeman said to Mr. Covington.

"Officer," Mr. Covington said, "I'm trying to run a legitimate business. I'm a law-abiding citizen and I pay my taxes, out of which, I might say, you obtain your salary. I have already tried to reach Mr. Safferty by telephone. The telephone appears to be out of order. I cannot leave my shop in the middle of the day to go looking for him."

Homer looked at Mr. Covington straight in the eye and placed a wagging finger under his nose. "You go get the inventor of this torture machine," he said, "and get my brother out of it. That's all."

"It's not a torture machine," Mr. Covington said. "It's the most improved animal trap on the market. It holds the animal aloft without damage to fur or body. No squeezing, cutting or crushing. It operates on the principle of dislocating the animal from its base and thereby rendering it powerless. Beside, Mr. Safferty may not be at home."

"Ah," Homer said, "what are you talking about?"

Now the policeman decided to study the trap. "Maybe," he suggested, "we'd better *saw* the boy out."

"Saw steel?" Mr. Covington said. "How?"

"Ulysses," Homer said, "do you want anything? Are you all right?"

Big Chris, working hard over the trap, looked from one brother to the other, deeply moved by the calm of the boy in the trap and the furious devotion of his brother.

"Ulysses," Homer said, "can I get you anything?"

"Papa," Ulysses said.

"Ah," Homer said, "can I get you anything besides Papa?"

"Marcus," the boy in the trap said.

"Marcus is in the Army," Homer said. "Do you want an ice cream cone or anything like that?"

"No," Ulysses said, "just Marcus."

"Well, Marcus is in the Army," Homer said. He turned to Covington. "Get my brother out of this thing and hurry up about it, too!"

"Wait a minute," Big Chris said. "Hold your brother there, boy! Don't let him fall!" Big Chris was very busy with the trap now.

"You're *breaking* the trap!" Mr. Covington said. "It's the only one of its kind in the world. You mustn't break it! I'll go get Mr. Safferty. You're wrecking a great invention. Mr. Safferty's an old man. He may never be able to make another trap like this. The boy's all right. He's unhurt. I'll go get Mr. Safferty. I'll only be an hour or two"

"An hour or two!" Homer shouted. He looked at Mr. Covington with the most terrible contempt in the world, and then all around at the store. "I'll break this whole store," he said. He looked back at Big Chris. "Go ahead, mister. Break the trap—break it!"

Big Chris tugged at the trap with every muscle in his fingers, arms, shoulders and back, and little by little the trap began to give way to the force of his strength.

Ulysses twisted around to watch the man. At last Big Chris destroyed the trap.

Ulysses was free.

Holding him so that he would not fall on his face, Homer set his little brother on his feet. The crowd in front of the store cheered, but not effectively, as they were unorganized and had no leader. Ulysses tried out his legs. As everything seemed to be all right now, Homer put his arms around his brother. Ulysses looked at Big Chris. The big man was almost exhausted.

"Somebody's got to pay for that trap," Mr. Covington said. "It's ruined. Somebody's got to pay for it."

Without a word, Big Chris brought some currency out of his pocket, counted out twenty dollars and tossed it onto the counter. He took Ulysses by the head and rubbed the boy's hair, as a father sometimes does. Then he turned and walked out of the store.

Homer talked to his brother. "Are you all right? How do you get into these terrible things?" Homer looked at the ruined trap and then kicked it.

"Careful there, boy," the policeman said. "That's some kind of a new invention. There's no telling what it's liable to do."

Mr. Covington went out into the street to speak to the people. "The store is open for business again. Covington's opens at eight every morning, closes at seven every night, except Saturdays when we are open till ten. Closed all day Sunday. Everything in the sporting line. Fishing tackle, guns, ammunition, and athletic goods. We're open for business, ladies and gentlemen. Come right in."

The people slowly walked away.

Homer turned to the policeman before leaving the store. "Who was that man that got my brother out of the trap?"

"Never saw the man before in my life," the policeman said.

"Big Chris," Ulysses said to Homer.

"Is that his name—Big Chris?"

"Yes. Big Chris."

Now, Auggie ran into the store. He looked at Ulysses. "Did you get out, Ulysses? How did you get out, Ulysses?"

"Big Chris," Ulysses said.

"How did he get out, Homer?" Auggie said. "What happened? What happened to the trap? Where's the big man with the beard? What happened while I was gone?"

"Everything's all right, Auggie," Homer said. "Did you tell Mr. Spangler what I told you?"

"Yeah, I told him. What happened, Homer? Does the trap work? Will it catch animals?"

"Ah," Homer said, "that trap's a lot of hooey. What good is it to catch an animal if you can't get it out? Mr. Covington, you got a lot of nerve charging Big Chris twenty dollars for a piece of junk like that."

"Twenty dollars is the standard price," Mr. Covington said.

"Standard price?" Homer said. "What are you talking about? Come on, Auggie, let's get out of here." The three boys left the store and walked to the telegraph office. Mr. Spangler was leaning on the counter, looking out at the street. Mr. Grogan was sending a telegram. Homer was limping worse than ever now from his collision with Mr. Byfield in the two-twenty low hurdle race.

"Mr. Spangler," he said, "this is my brother Ulysses. We just got him out of some kind of a trap over at Covington's. Big Chris got him out. He had to break the trap. And then he had to pay for it—twenty dollars. This is Auggie. Did he tell you why I'm late?"

"Everything's all right," Spangler said. "A few telegrams have piled up that you've got to deliver, but it's all right. So that's your brother—Ulysses?" Ulysses was standing behind the telegraph operator, watching him work. In front of the telegraph operator, across the table, Auggie stood, listening to the telegraph box.

"A few calls have come in, too," Spangler said. "I took a

couple of the near ones myself. The other two are on the call sheet. Take the calls first, then deliver the telegrams."

"Yes, sir," Homer said. "Right away. I'm awfully sorry about this, Mr. Spangler. Will you mind Ulysses until I get back? Maybe a little later when things are quiet I can take him home on my wheel."

"I'll mind your brother," Spangler said. "You go ahead."

"Yes, sir," Homer said. "Thanks very much. Ulysses won't be any trouble. He'll just watch. He won't *do* anything."

Homer left the telegraph office, limping in a hurry.

14. Diana

ULYSSES MOVED CLOSER to Mr. Grogan while Auggie listened to the clatter of the telegraph box.

"What's that for?" Auggie said to Mr. Spangler, indicating the box.

"Mr. Grogan's sending a telegram."

"Where's he sending it to?"

"New York."

"All the way to New York? How does it go?"

"It goes by wire."

"Wires on telegraph poles? Telegraph poles from here to New York? All the way from Ithaca to New York?"

"That's right."

"Who sends 'em?"

"All sorts of people."

The newsboy thought a moment and then said, "I never got a telegram in my life. How do you get one?"

"Somebody sends you one."

"I never got one. Who would send it?"

"Some friend or somebody."

"Everybody I know is right here in Ithaca." A green light went on, on the repeater rack. "What's that green light for?" Auggie said.

"It's a signal to us that the line is clear," Spangler said.

"What line?"

"The line to San Francisco."

"Oh, " Auggie said. "How old do you have to be to be a messenger?"

"Sixteen."

"I'm nine. What do you have to wait so long for? You can enlist in the Navy when you're seventeen."

"It's a rule."

"What have they got all them rules for all the time?" Auggie said.

Spangler began to file a batch of outgoing telegrams into a block of pigeonholes.

"Well," he said, "*that* rule is to keep children from working."

"Why?"

"So they won't get tired. So they can play. That rule is for the protection of children."

"Protection from what?"

"Well," Spangler said, "protection from bosses who make kids do too much work for the money they're paid."

"Well, what if the kid doesn't want to be protected? What if he *wants* to work?"

"The rule protects him anyway."

"How old do you have to be not to be a child any more? How old do you have to be to protect yourself, or to do any kind of work you want to do?"

"Got to be sixteen to be a messenger."

"Homer's working, isn't he? Since when is Homer sixteen?"

"Well," Spangler said, "Homer is an exception. He's only fourteen but he's strong and he's intelligent."

"What do you mean—intelligent?" Auggie said. "Do you have to be intelligent to be a messenger?"

"No, but it helps. It helps to be intelligent no matter what you are."

"Well, how can you tell if a man's intelligent?"

Spangler looked at the newsboy and smiled. "By talking to him a few minutes."

"What are you putting those papers in there for?"

"These are telegrams that were sent yesterday. We file them in here, city by city, for our records and our bookkeeping. Now this telegram is to San Francisco, so I put it in here. All these telegrams in here are to San Francisco."

"I can do that," Auggie said. "I can ride a bike, too—only I haven't got a bike. If I get a bike, Mr. Spangler, can I be a messenger, too? Will you give me a job?"

Spangler stopped working to look at the boy. "Yes, I will, Auggie, but not just yet. Nine isn't quite old enough. Thirteen or fourteen—yes."

"Twelve maybe?" Auggie said.

"Maybe. What do you want to be a messenger for?"

"Learn things. Read telegrams. Find out about things." He paused a moment. "I won't be twelve for three years."

"Three years will go by in no time at all."

"Doesn't seem like it. I've been waiting a long time already."

"You'll find out," Spangler said. "You'll be twelve before you know it. What's your last name?"

"Gottlieb. I'm August Gottlieb."

The manager of the telegraph office and the newsboy looked at each other, each of them very earnest and very serious. "August Gottlieb," Spangler said, "I give you my word. When the time comes—"

Spangler stopped speaking to behold a young woman named Diana Steed who came galloping into the office. In front of the office in the street was the automobile which had brought her. At the wheel of the automobile sat a chauffeur in uniform. In a special, somewhat artificial yet attractive voice, she cried out to Spangler, "Oh, there you are, darling!" She charged upon him with a sweet fury of affection, threw her arms around him, and kissed him in a way that was so incredible it might have been real, or a little better than real.

"Wait a minute!" Spangler said. He held her back, and put the wire basket he was holding on the desk. The young woman came for him but again he warded her off. "Wait a minute," he said. "This is August Gottlieb!"

"How do you do, little boy?" the young woman said.

"August," Spangler said, "this is Miss Steed."

"Hello," August said. And then, not knowing what else to say, he said, "Paper, lady?"

"Why, yes, of course," Diana said. "How much is it?"

"Five cents," Auggie said. "Home edition. Race results, stock market closings, and the latest news of the War."

"I'll take one, please," Diana said.

Auggie accepted the nickel and handed Miss Steed a paper which he first folded in a very efficient and businesslike way, whacking the full paper on his knee, folding it in half, whacking the half paper on his knee again, folding that in half, and then, turning the result around neatly, somewhat like a magician doing an important trick. "Thank you, ma'am," he said. "Wednesdays I sell *The Saturday Evening Post*. I work the whole town."

"Well," Diana said, "I hope you make a lot of money."

"I average about forty cents a day, papers and magazines both. When the County Fair opens I sell soda pop."

"Well, you *do* keep busy, *don't* you?" Diana said in her bubbling cheerful voice.

"Yes," Auggie said, "and I learn things, too. I can figure people out pretty good." It appeared that Auggie had figured out Miss Steed and was pleased with his conclusions.

"Yes, you do," she said, "I'm sure you do." She turned to Spangler. "I waited for your call, darling. You *did* say you would call at five, didn't you?"

"Oh, yes," Spangler said. "I forgot. I was talking to Auggie here. He wants to be a messenger and I've just told him when the time comes he's going to have a job."

"Well, thanks, Mr. Spangler," Auggie said. He moved to go. "I'll be seeing you. Good-by, ma'am. Good-by, Ulysses."

"Ulysses!" Diana said to Spangler "My, what an appropriate name! Ulysses in Ithaca! Darling, I've only a moment. You will be out for dinner, won't you? You *must*, you know."

Spangler began to speak but the young woman stopped him. "No, you *promised!* Yes, you did! Mother and Father are dying to meet you! Seven o'clock sharp!"

"Now, wait a minute," Spangler said.

"Darling," Diana said, "you can't disappoint me again, can you?"

Spangler sighed. "I've been out to dinner twice in my life. I was scared to death both times, and I had no fun at all."

"You'll *love* Mother and Father. We're not dressing—just evening clothes."

"Evening clothes? I'm wearing the clothes I wear day and night both."

"Seven o'clock," Diana said. She noticed the hard-boiled egg on Spangler's desk. "Oh, darling, what a clever paper weight! What is it?"

"It's an egg, I keep it for luck."

"How sweet!" Diana said. "I've got to run, darling." She gave him a quick farewell kiss and left the office.

Mr. Grogan finished typing a telegram. Spangler led Ulysses over to the old man. "Willie," he said, "I'm going over to Corbett's for a drink. This is Ulysses Macauley, Homer's little brother. He's had an experience of some sort. Got caught in some kind of trap. Ulysses, this is Mr. Willie Grogan."

"Oh, we're old friends," Mr. Grogan said. "He's been watching me work."

"One drink and I'll be right back," Spangler said.

15. The Girl on the Corner

SPANGLER TURNED to go, but he was stopped by the working of the call box—by the message which simultaneously rang out and printed itself upon the ticker tape. He went to the instrument on the delivery desk and studied the marks on the tape. "That's a call from Ithaca Wine," he said to Grogan—"away out in the sticks. If Homer comes in, keep him here until we get the regular evening call from Sunripe Raisin. He's beat Western Union there twice in two tries. If he can make it again today we may have a pretty good

month of business after all. How many telegrams did we
get from them yesterday?"

"Sixty-seven," Grogan said.

"Sixty-seven telegrams out of sixty-eight," Spangler said.
"First boy there gets all the telegrams but one. Second boy
gets one. Well, I'll go get that drink."

But now another call began to come in: *Dot dot dash
dot dot dot.* When the manager of the telegraph office had
heard only the first two dots, he knew the call was from
Sunripe Raisin, and as Homer was not in the office to take
the call, he shouted to Grogan. *"I'll take the call. I'll get
there first myself."*

By the time the call was repeated three times, Spangler
was in the middle of the next block, moving through the
people like an open field runner in a football game. On the
corner before him, thirty yards away, stood a shy, lonely-
looking girl of eighteen or nineteen—tired, hushed, and
therefore beautiful. She was waiting for a bus to take her
home, after work. Even though he was running, it was impossible for Spangler not to notice the girl's isolation—
which seemed to him, even though he was in a hurry, like
the isolation of *all* things, one from another. Not clown-
ing, without any premeditation, swiftly and easily, he
reached the girl, paused a moment, and kissed her on the
cheek. Before he moved on, he told her the only thing it
was possible to say: "You are the loveliest woman in the
world!"

He ran on. When he was going up the steps of the Sunripe Raisin Association three at a time, the Western Union
messenger, off to a slow start because the delivery clerk did
not know the calls by heart as Spangler did, was just getting off his bicycle in front of the building, and when Spangler was going into the office, the Western Union messenger had only begun to wait for the elevator.

As if he were still a messenger, Spangler announced
himself to the old woman at the desk of Sunripe Raisin.
"Postal Telegraph!" he said.

"Tom!" the old woman said, pleased and surprised.
"Don't tell me you're a *messenger* now, too."

"Once a messenger, always a messenger," Spangler said, not at all embarassed by the meaninglessness of the remark. He smiled at the old woman and then said, "But most of all I came to see *you*, Mrs. Brockington."

The Western Union messenger came into the office. "Western Union," he said.

"Well, Harry," Mrs. Brockington said, "you've been beaten again." She handed the messenger one telegram. "Better luck next time."

The Western Union boy, a little confused and embarassed because he had been beaten again, this time not by another messenger but by the manager of the Postal Telegraph office, took the one telegram and said, "Thanks just the same, Mrs. Brockington," and left the office.

The old woman handed Spangler a whole bundle of telegrams. "Here you are, Tom. One hundred and twenty-nine night letters—all over the country—all paid. But where's the new messenger?"

"Homer?" Spangler said. "Homer Macauley? We got slowed down this afternoon on account of an accident that happened to his little brother, Ulysses. Got caught in some kind of a trap at Covington's. Homer had to go and get him out. But you'll be seeing him from now on." He smiled at the old woman. "Thanks for the telegrams."

When he reached the corner where the isolated girl had stood, he paused a moment. "It was right here that she stood. I'll never see her again, most likely, but even if I do, I'll never see her again as she was when I saw her this afternoon." He moved on down the street, whistling to himself. When he was across the street from Corbett's, he heard pianola music—the old waltz called *All That I Want Is You*. He moved to the swinging doors of the saloon, listened a moment, then went in. Corbett himself was at the bar and immediately went to work, getting Spangler his regular Scotch and plain water. He glanced over at the three soldiers listening to the player piano. "How is it going, Ralph?"

"Not bad," Corbett said. "Soldiers with a lot of time to kill and not very much money. I buy them three to their one."

"Can you afford to do that?" Spangler said.

"No, but what's the difference? After the War maybe I'll get some of it back. I just can't be a bartender. I'm Young Corbett."

The manager of the telegraph office and the former prize fighter talked for five minutes and then Spangler went back to the office.

16. Going Home

AT THE DELIVERY desk he saw the Macauley brothers, Homer and Ulysses—the messenger folding telegrams and putting them in envelopes, the younger brother watching with quiet admiration.

"Did *you* get Sunripe Raisin, Mr. Spangler?" Homer said.

"Yes, I did," Spangler said. "One hundred and twenty-nine telegrams." He showed the telegrams to the messenger.

"One hundred and twenty-nine! How did you get there first?"

"I ran."

"You beat Western Union to Sunripe Raisin *running?*"

"Sure. Nothing to it. I even stopped on the way—to pay tribute to beauty and innocence." Homer didn't understand, but Spangler went right on. "Take Ulysses home."

"Yes, sir," Homer said. "We've got a call from Guggenheim's. It's down our way, so I'll hike Ulysses home, then go to Guggenheim's and from there I'll go to Ithaca Wine, then Foley's, and then I'll come right back. I'll be back in no time." The messenger left the office and carefully set his brother on the handlebars of his bicycle while Spangler watched. The older brother swung onto the bike and began to pedal down the street. When they were out of the town itself, Ulysses twisted around to look at his brother. For the first time that day his face broke out with the Macauley smile.

"Homer?"

"What?"

"I can sing."

"That's good."

Ulysses began to sing. "We will sing one song." He stopped and began again. "We will sing one song," but again he stopped.

"That's not a song. That's just a little part of a song. Now, you listen to me, and then sing with me." The older brother began to sing while the younger brother listened.

> "Weep no more, my lady, O weep no more today
> We will sing one song for the old Kentucky home
> For the old Kentucky home far away"

"Sing it again, Homer," Ulysses said.

"O.K.," Homer said, and began to sing again, but this time the younger brother sang with the older, and as they sang Ulysses saw the freight train again with the Negro leaning over the side of the gondola, smiling and waving. That was one of the greatest things that had ever happened to Ulysses Macauley in his four years of life in the world.

He waved to a man and the man waved back to *him*—not once, but many times. He would remember that as long as he lived.

Homer got off his bicycle in front of the Macauley house and carefully set Ulysses on his feet. They stood together a moment, listening to the harp and piano of their mother and sister and the singing of their neighbor, Mary Arena.

"All right," Homer said, "you're home now. Go on in. I've got to go on to work."

"Going to work?" Ulysses said.

"Yes," Homer said, "but I'll be home tonight. Go on in, Ulysses."

The younger brother started up the front porch steps. When he got to the door, the older brother began to ride on down the street.

17. Three Soldiers

WHEN THE STEED FAMILY and their guests, including Thomas Spangler, sat down to dinner, a heavy rain was falling over Ithaca. Bess Macauley and Mary Arena, in raincoats and galoshes, walked to the telegraph office, bearing Homer's lunch-box. As they passed the Owl Drug Store, a young man standing in the doorway gave them the old wolf eye.

"Hi-ya, pretty," he said to Bess. "What's with?"

Bess ignored the young man and moved closer to Mary as they went up the street. Now, coming toward them were three young soldiers. They were sporting around in the street at a game improvised out of their happiness at being free for the night, and out of the refreshing rain. They pushed and chased one another, roaring with laughter, and calling out the nicknames they had given one another—Fat, Texas, and Horse. When the three boys saw Mary and Bess they came to a worshipful halt. They bowed very low, one after another. The girls were pleased, but they weren't sure what they ought to do—what attitude they ought to take.

"They're just soldiers, Bess," Mary whispered—"away from home."

"Let's stop," Bess said.

The soldier called Fat stepped forward as the official representative of the group.

"American girls," he said, "we of the great Democratic Army, your humble servants, the soldiers—here today and, we hope, here tomorrow—thank you for your beautiful faces, in times of dryness no less than in times of rain, such as the present. May I present my comrades and your devoted admirers. This is Texas—he's from New Jersey. This is Horse—he's from Texas. And I'm Fat—I'm from hunger. Now, more than anything else I hunger for the companionship of beautiful American girls. How about it?"

"Well," Bess said, "we were going to the Kinema."

"To the Kinema!" Fat said dramatically. "May we—soldiers—whether here today or gone tomorrow—accompany you—American girls—to the Kinema? Tonight is tonight and tomorrow is tomorrow, but tomorrow we return to barracks, to the awful but unavoidable business of war. Tonight we are your brothers—far from our firesides, and lonely, for Ithaca is not our native land. I have waddled into this costume of the American soldier from the side streets of the ferocious city of Chicago, of the old nation of Illinois. Restore me to that city and to that nation tonight in memory, and restore my good brothers each to his good place, for we are of one family, and except for the war we might never meet." The soldier who was called Fat bowed, then stood upright. "What is your decision?"

"Is he crazy?" Mary whispered.

"No," Bess said, "he's just lonely. Let's go to the movie with them."

"All right," Mary said, "but you *tell* him. I don't know what to say."

Bess smiled at the soldier. "All right," she said.

"Thank you, American girls," Fat said. He offered his arm to Bess.

"First, I've got to take my brother his lunch, at the telegraph office."

"Telegraph?" Fat said. "Then I shall send a telegram." He turned to the others. "How about you, Texas?"

"How much does it cost to send a telegram to New Jersey?" Texas said.

"Not nearly as much as it's worth," Fat said. "Horse?"

"Yeah," Horse said. "I think I'd like to send a telegram to Ma and Joe and Kitty—that's my girl," he said to Bess.

"Every girl in the world is *my* girl," Fat said, "and as I cannot send telegrams to each of them, I shall send a telegram to only one. I shall send millions of telegrams to the only one."

Willie Grogan was alone in the office when the two young women and the three soldiers walked in. The old man stood behind the counter.

"I'm Homer's sister Bess. I've brought his lunch." She put the box on the counter.

"Your brother will be in soon, Miss Macauley," Grogan said. "I'll see that he gets his lunch."

"And these boys want to send telegrams," Bess said.

"Very well, young men," Grogan said. "Help yourself to telegraph blanks and pencils."

"How much does it cost to send a telegram to Jersey City?" Texas said.

"Twenty-five words for fifty cents, plus a small tax. But don't count the address or the signature. The telegram will be delivered tomorrow morning."

"Fifty cents? That's not bad at all." Texas began to write his telegram.

"How much does it cost to San Antone?" Horse said.

"Half as much as to Jersey City. San Antonio is nearer Ithaca than Jersey City."

The soldier called Fat who had been busy writing his telegram now handed it to the old man. Grogan read the telegram as he counted it.

EMMA DANA
C/O THE UNIVERSITY OF CHICAGO
CHICAGO, ILLINOIS
MY DARLING, I LOVE YOU, I MISS YOU, I THINK OF YOU ALWAYS. KEEP WRITING. KEEP STUDYING. KEEP WAITING. KEEP BELIEVING. DON'T FORGET ME. DON'T EVER FORGET ME BECAUSE I AM THE ONE WHO WILL NEVER FORGET YOU.
                                                        NORMAN

Next, the soldier called Texas handed Grogan *his* telegram.

MRS. EDITH ANTHONY
1702½ WILMINGTON STREET
JERSEY CITY, NEW JERSEY
DEAR MA. HOW ARE YOU? I AM FINE. I GOT YOUR LETTER AND THE BOX OF DRIED FIGS. THANKS. DON'T WORRY ABOUT ANYTHING. SO LONG. LOVE.
                                                        BERNARD

Then, the soldier called Horse handed the old telegraph operator *his* telegram.

MRS. HARVEY GUILFORD
211 SANDYFORD BOULEVARD
SAN ANTONIO, TEXAS
HELLO MA. JUST WANT TO SAY HELLO FROM ITHACA IN SUNNY CALIFORNIA. ONLY IT'S RAINING. HA HA. GIVE MY REGARDS TO EVERYBODY. TELL JOE HE CAN HAVE MY GUN AND SHELLS. LOVE.
                                                        QUENTIN

The soldiers and the girls left the office and Mr. Grogan went to his table to send the telegrams.

On the screen at the Kinema Theatre, as the three soldiers and the two American girls walked down the center aisle, Mr. Winston Churchill, Prime Minister of England in the year of our Lord 1942, appeared before the Canadian House of Parliament. By the time the young people were seated, Mr. Churchill had said three things, one after another, which had caused increasing delight both to the members of the Canadian House of Parliament and to the members of the audience at the Kinema Theatre in Ithaca. The soldier called Fat leaned over to Bess Macauley.

"There," he said, "is one of the great men of our time—and a great American, too."

"I thought Churchill was an Englishman," Horse said.

"Sure," Fat said, "but he's an American, too." He moved just a little closer to the girl on the other side of him, Mary Arena. "Thanks a lot for letting us come to the movie with you," he said. "It feels better to have girls near. It *smells* better than just soldiers."

"We were coming to the movie anyway," Mary said.

Now, the man named Franklin Delano Roosevelt, President of the United States, appeared in the newsreel, making a radio speech to the nation from his home in Hyde Park. He spoke with his usual mixture of solemnity and humor. The five young people listened carefully. When the speech was over the American flag appeared on the screen and everybody in the theatre began to applaud.

"I get a lump in my throat every time I see the flag," Bess said. "It used to make me think of Washington and Lincoln, but now it makes me think of my brother Marcus. He's a soldier, too."

"Oh, you've got a brother in the Army?" Fat said.

"He was somewhere in North Carolina the last time we heard from him," Bess said.

At that moment Marcus stood at the bar in a saloon called The Dive Bomber in a small town in North Carolina. His friend Tobey George and three other soldiers were at the bar with him. Marcus was playing a song called *A Dream*, and Tobey was singing. After the song, Tobey sat down beside his friend Marcus and asked him to talk some more about Ithaca and the Macauleys there.

As Marcus Macauley began to tell Tobey George about Ithaca, Thomas Spangler and Diana Steed came down the aisle of the Kinema Theatre. Now, the feature picture began to appear on the screen. When they were seated the screen was filling with words, not pictures. These words named the picture and the people who had helped to make the picture. There were vast numbers of words, an enormous amount of credit given to enormous numbers of people. Accompanying these credits was a majestically inappropriate theme of music which had been especially composed for the occasion.

Spangler and Diana sat very close to the screen, in the third row, ten rows in front of Bess and Mary and the three soldiers. Their seats were at the very center of a row whose only other occupants were small boys. Now on the screen appeared the spick and span linoleum-floored hall of a hospital. Over a loud-speaker at the end of the hall came the harsh voice of a bitter nurse who spoke over-emphatically.

"Dr. Cavanagh!" she cried. "Surgery! Dr. Cavanagh! Surgery!"

Immediately upon hearing these words Thomas Spangler got to his feet. He had had a few to drink and the evening had been a rather difficult if pleasant one for him, full of complications and potentialities which were now working themselves out, it seemed, so that he felt no need at all not to carry on as if he himself were no older than the others in that row of seats.

"Ooop!" he said. "Wrong movie!" He took Diana's hand and said, "Come on."

"But, darling, the movie isn't over yet!" Diana whispered.

Spangler dragged her along. "It's over for *me*. Come on." Now, they were passing a small boy who was watching the screen with total fascination.

"*You'll* get to Heaven," Spangler said to the boy, and then to Diana, "Come on, don't stand in the boy's way."

"What did you say, mister?" the boy said.

"Heaven!" Spangler said. "I say *you'll* get there."

"Have you got the time?"

"No, I haven't, but it's still early."

"Yes, sir," the boy said.

Now, Spangler and Diana were in the aisle.

"We'll go to Corbett's," Spangler said. "Have a couple of drinks, listen to the pianola, and then you can go home." He turned to face the screen and began walking backward.

"Look at Dr. Cavanagh," he said. "He's going to pull out one of his front teeth with a pair of pliers."

In the lobby of the theater, Diana said, "You do love me, don't you?"

"Love you?" Spangler said. "I took you to a movie, didn't I?"

They went out to the street and began hurrying toward Corbett's, moving close to the buildings in order to keep out of the rain.

18. The Telegram

As SPANGLER and Diana ran through the rain towards
Corbett's, Homer Macauley, soaking wet, brought his bicycle to a stop in front of the telegraph office and went in.
He looked over the situation at the delivery desk. There
were no calls to take, but there was one telegram to deliver.

Mr. Grogan finished a telegram he was typing and got
up. "Your sister Bess brought your lunch, my boy."

"Ah, she didn't need to bring any lunch. I was going to
get us two pies." Homer took the box and said, "There's

enough of it. Will you have some lunch with me, Mr. Grogan?"

"Thank you, my boy, I'm not hungry."

"Maybe if you start to eat a little, your appetite will improve, Mr. Grogan."

"No. Thanks very much. But you're soaking wet. Look here, we've got raincoats."

"I got *caught* in the rain." Homer bit into a sandwich. "I'll eat this sandwich, and then I'll deliver the telegram." He chewed a moment and then looked over at the old telegraph operator. "What kind of a telegram is it?"

From the way that Mr. Grogan didn't answer, Homer knew the telegram was another death message. He stopped chewing and gulped the food down, dry. "I wish I didn't have to deliver telegrams like this," he said.

"Yes, I know," Mr. Grogan said. He didn't speak again for half a minute, while the messenger held the unfinished sandwich in his hand. "Your sister was with another very pretty girl."

"That's Mary. She's Marcus's girl. They're going to be married after the War."

"They were with three soldiers who sent telegrams."

"Is that so? Can I see the telegrams?"

Mr. Grogan indicated the hook on which dispatched telegrams were placed. Homer took the telegrams off the hook and one by one read them. After having read them, he looked at the old telegraph operator.

"If a fellow dies that way, Mr. Grogan," he said, "somebody you know, or somebody you don't know, somebody you've never even seen—they don't just die for nothing, do they?"

The old telegraph operator waited a moment before speaking, and then, as if there was so much to say that he wouldn't be able to make it alone, he went to the drawer of his table and got out the bottle. He took a good long swig, sat down, and tried to decide what to say.

"I've been a long time in the world," he said, "but I don't know the answer to that question, my boy. I'm not even sure there is an answer. It's a young question, and I'm an old man."

Mr. Grogan sighed deeper than ever now and then after a moment brought out a slip of paper from his vest pocket, which he handed to the messenger. "Will you go on an errand for me again, to the drug store?"

Homer nodded, and hurried out of the office.

Mr. Grogan stood alone in the telegraph office, looking around at everything with a strange affection mixed with a kind of loving anger. Almost slowly he clutched at his collar, as if he had been waiting too long for the swift attack that could no longer surprise him. He moved back to his chair and sat in a terrible stiffness until the attack had spent its most extreme force.

The messenger returned from the drug store and handed the telegraph operator the small box.

"Water," the old man said.

Homer filled a paper cup full of water and took it to the old man, who dumped three of the pills out of the little box, tossed them into his mouth, took the cup from Homer, and swallowed the pills.

"Thank you, my boy."

Homer watched the old man to see if he was going to be all right, then went to the delivery desk and took up the telegram of death. He stood a moment holding the telegram and looking at it, and then he opened the envelope and took the message out of it, to read. He put the telegram back into a new envelope, sealed it, and then turned and walked out of the office into the rain. The old telegraph operator got up out of his chair and followed the boy into the street. He stood there on the sidewalk and watched the boy push against the wind and the rain. Inside the office the telegraph box began to rattle, but the old man didn't hear. The telephone rang, but again the old man didn't hear. He did not turn and go back into the office until the telephone and had rung seven times.

19. Alan

FIFTEEN MINUTES LATER Homer got off his bicycle in front of a large fine old house where a party was in progress. Through the windows he could see four young couples dancing. The boy felt sick and terrified. He went up the walk to the door and stood listening to the music. He moved a finger toward the door bell and then let his hand drop.

"I'll go back to the office," he said to himself. "I'll quit."

He sat down on the steps of the house, to think. After a long time he got up and went to the door again and pressed his finger against the button. When the door opened he saw a young woman, and before he knew what he was doing he turned and ran to his bicycle. The young woman came out on the porch and called out, "Why, what's the matter, boy?"

Homer got off his bicycle and ran back to the porch. "I'm sorry," he said quickly. "I've got a telegram for Mrs. Claudia Beaufrere."

"Of course. It's Mother's birthday," the young woman said. She stepped back into the hallway. "Mother," she called out, "here's a telegram for you."

The girl's mother came to the door. "It's from Alan, I'm sure," she said. "Come in, young man. You must have a piece of my birthday cake."

"No, thank you, ma'am," Homer said. "I've got to go back to work." He held the telegram out to the woman, who took it as if it were nothing more than a birthday greeting.

"Not until you've had a piece of cake and a glass of punch." She tugged at Homer's arm and dragged him into the room to a table loaded with cake and sandwiches and punch. The music and dancing continued. "It's my birthday," she said. "Lord, I *am* old. Well, you must wish me happiness, boy." She handed Homer a glass of punch.

"I wish you—" Homer began to say, but he couldn't go on. He put the glass of punch on the table and bolted to the door. The mother looked around the room, then went to one side where she wouldn't be noticed, and the daughter, watching her, moved to the other side. Homer was on his bicycle racing through the rain back to the telegraph office. On the wall of the hall, in front of the mother, was a framed picture of a good-looking red-headed boy. Written on the photograph were the words, "To Mother with love from Alan on his 12th birthday." The mother opened the telegram and read it, while the phonograph continued with a song called *Chanson pour Ma Brune,* and the happy people continued to dance. The daughter looked across the room at her mother in the hallway. Almost as if she had lost her reason, she rushed to the phonograph and turned it off.

"Mother!" she cried, and ran toward the woman in the hallway.

20. After the Movie

Now, THE KINEMA THEATRE was letting out its visitors after the last show. In the street Bess turned to the soldier called Fat and said, "Well, we must go home now."

"Thank you, American girls," Fat said. It was time to say good-by, and yet somehow they stood together in the street, waiting, as if something wonderful but unknowable was on the verge of happening. The soldier called Fat looked from Bess to Mary, and then easily and innocently kissed Bess, and then Mary.

Now, the soldier called Horse shouted, "Well, what

about us? We're somebody, too. We're in the Army, too."
So this soldier kissed the girls, too. And after him Texas
kissed them. A woman in the street watched with bitter dis-
taste. The girls turned quickly and hurried down the street.
The soldier called Horse jumped, and then pushed the soldier called Texas, who jumped and pushed the soldier
called Fat. They moved down the side street, shouting at
one another.

"Waaa-hooo!" Horse shouted.

"How you talk!" Texas shouted at Fat. "How you *do*
talk!"

The soldier called Fat cackled with delight.

"Oh man!" he shouted. "When I get to Congress! I'll tell
them a thing or two."

"Yippee-aye-ay," Horse shouted. *"Git along little dogies
—it's your misfortune and none of my own."*

Now, the three soldiers began leaping over one another
at a swift game of leap-frog, pushing down the dark, wet
street nearer and nearer to whatever the hell might be next
for each of them, God-helping.

21. Valley Champion for Kids

BY THE TIME the messenger got back to the telegraph office from the Beaufrere home, the rain had stopped, the moon was shining, and an empty and exhausted cluster of clouds, now white, was being driven across the sky. The messenger was very tired when he came limping into the office.

"What's the matter with your leg?" Mr. Grogan said. "You've been limping all day."

"It's nothing," Homer said. "Any more telegrams?"

"All clear, and soon you can go home to bed. Now tell me. What happened to your leg?"

"I guess I twisted a ligament or something, running the two-twenty low hurdles this afternoon. Mr. Spangler was Valley Champion of that race, and I guess I'd like to be Valley Champion some day myself, too. I don't think I'll be able to make it this year, though." Homer flexed his leg a couple of times. "I'll rub some Sloan's Liniment on it tonight. Is the limp noticeable?"

"Well," Mr. Grogan said, "it's not *too* noticeable, but it is a *little*. Can you ride your bike all right?"

"Sure," Homer said. "It hurts a little when I get the hurt leg up, so I try to do all the pumping with my right leg. Sometimes I take the left leg off the pedal and let it hang. That way it rests. I guess something's happened to the ligament—I'll rub it with liniment."

There was a pause. Then the old telegraph operator said, "Keep talking, my boy."

"Oh, I *want* to, all right, but I don't know where to start," Homer said. "I didn't know *anything* until I got this job. I knew a lot of things, but I didn't know the half of it, and maybe I never will, either. Maybe nobody ever will. If anybody *should*, though, I should. I *want* to know, and I'll *always* want to know, and I guess I'll always keep trying, but how can you ever know? How can any man ever really get it all straight so that it makes sense?"

"Well, Mr. Grogan said, "I don't know, but I'm glad you've made up your mind to keep trying."

"I've *got* to keep trying," Homer said. "I don't know how it is with other people, and I don't know whether I can tell you this or not, but I'm not just the guy people *see*, I'm somebody else besides—somebody better. Sometimes *I* don't even know what to make of it. I'd be ashamed to say this to anybody but you, Mr. Grogan, but some day I'm going to go to work and do something for the kids everywhere. All kinds of kids having all kinds of trouble. I don't know what it's going to be, but it's going to be *something*. Decent, I mean." Homer tested his leg to see if it had become healed as he had talked. It hadn't. "I don't like the way things are, Mr. Grogan. I don't know why, but I want them to be better. I guess it's because I think they *ought* to be better. At school I say a lot of funny things, but I don't do it to make trouble for the teachers. I do it because I've got to. Everybody's so mixed up, and everything's so wrong that I've just got to say funny things once in a while. I guess we ought to have some fun out of being alive. I don't think I could act refined even if I wanted to. I couldn't be polite if I didn't mean it."

He flexed his leg again and spoke of it as if it weren't his own. "Something's the matter with it." He glanced up at the clock. "Well, Mr. Grogan, it's five minutes after twelve. I guess I'll go home. I don't feel very sleepy, though, and tomorrow's Saturday. Saturday used to be the best day of all for me. No more, though. I guess I'll come down to the office. Maybe I can help out." He lifted the lunch-box off the delivery desk. "Wouldn't you like a sandwich now, Mr. Grogan?"

"Well," the old telegraph operator said, "come to think of it, my boy, yes, I would. I'm hungry now." Mr. Grogan took a sandwich out of the open box and bit into it. "Please thank your mother for me."

"Ah, it's nothing.

"No, please thank her for me."

"Yes, sir," Homer said, and left the office.

22. The Holdup Man

ALONE IN THE TELEGRAPH OFFICE, Mr. Grogan, once young, once the fastest telegraph operator in the world, slowly began to clear off the work table. He hummed softly to himself a theme which had stayed in his memory from the earliest days of his life. As the old man did his work, Thomas Spangler, fresh from Corbett's and a little under the influence of alcohol and a mixture of giddy and solemn happiness, came into the office and went to his desk. He glanced over at the old telegraph operator, but did not speak. They had an understanding. Very often it was no matter at all to be at work for an hour or two without exchanging one word. Spangler lifted the good-luck egg off a pile of telegrams and studied its amazing symmetry. Then he put the egg back on the pile of telegrams and, remembering the girl pleasantly, he puckered up his lips in order to speak as she was given to speaking.

"You do love me, don't you?"

The old telegraph operator glanced at the manager of the office.

"What's that, Tom?"

"Willie, what would you think of a young woman who everytime she sees you tells you: *'You do love me, don't you?'* "

"I'd probably wonder how in the world she ever found out."

"It's the same with me." Spangler rubbed his face as if to get over his happiness and then said, "Anything doing tonight?"

"About the same, except for the rain."

"How's the new messenger? Is he all right?"

"The best *I've* ever seen. What do *you* think of him?"

"I liked him from the time he came up and asked for a job," Spangler said. *"You do love me, don't you?"* He couldn't get over the extraordinary way Diana Steed spoke the small words. "You can go home now, Willie. I'll close the office. I've got a little work to do."

"Home?" Mr. Grogan said. "If you don't mind, Tom, I'd like to sit around a little while with you. I've got nothing to do after work except sleep, and I can't sleep. I guess I'm scared."

"No need to be scared, Willie. I'd be helpless in this Office without you. You'll live to be a hundred, and you'll work every day of your life."

"Thanks," the old telegraph operator said. He paused and then said softly, "I had another little attack tonight. Oh, nothing serious. I felt it coming on for some time. The boy was here. I sent him for the medicine. I'm supposed to see the doctor every day, but I'm afraid to see him. And I'm supposed to rest."

"Doctors don't know everything, but maybe you ought to rest a little anyway."

"Oh, I'll rest, I'll take the great rest, Tom."

"Go to Corbett's on the corner and have yourself a drink. Listen to the pianola. Come back and we'll talk over old times—Wolinsky and Tomlinson and old man Davenport. Harry Bull the lineman, crazy Fred McIntyre, and wonderful Jerry Beattie. Go ahead now, Willie. Have yourself a drink, and when you come back we'll kick around old times."

"I'm not supposed to drink, Tom."

"I know you're not *supposed* to, but I also know you *like* to, and what a man likes to do is sometimes more important than what he is supposed to do—so go ahead and have yourself a drink."

"All right, Tom," Mr. Grogan said, and left the office.

On the sidewalk for three or four minutes a young man had passed the office several times, looking in. He came in at last and stood at the counter. Spangler noticed him and went over.

"How are you?" Spangler said, remembering the boy. "I thought you'd be on your way home to Pennsylvania long ago. Your mother sent you the money. You didn't need to come back to pay me."

"I didn't come back to pay you," the young man said. "I came back to get more, and I didn't come to beg it, either. I came to *take* it."

"What's the matter with you?" Spangler said.

"This is what's the matter with me," the young man said. From his right-hand coat pocket he brought out a revolver and held it in a trembling hand. Spangler, still a little drunk, couldn't understand.

"Come on. Give me all the money you've got in this place. Everybody's killing everybody, so I don't mind if I kill you. And I don't mind if *I'm* killed, either. I'm excited and I don't want any trouble, so give me all the money, and hurry."

Spangler drew open the cash drawer and took the money out of the several compartments. He placed the money—currency, rolls of coin and open coins—on the counter before the boy.

"I'd give you the money, anyway," Spangler said, "but

not because you're pointing a gun at me. I'd give it to you because you need it. Here. This is all the money there is. Take it and get on a train and go home. Go back where you belong. I won't report a theft. I'll make it good myself. There's about seventy-five dollars there."

He waited for the boy to take the money, but the boy wouldn't touch it.

"I mean it," Spangler said. "Take the money and go— you need it. You're no criminal, and you're not so sick you can't get well. Your mother's waiting for you. This money is a gift from me to her. You won't be a thief taking it. Just take the money, put that gun away and go home. *Throw* the gun away—you'll feel better."

The young man put the gun back into his coat pocket. Over his trembling mouth he placed the hand which had held the gun. "I ought to go out and shoot myself," he said.

"Don't talk like a fool," Spangler said. He gathered the money together and held it out to the young man. "Now here. This is all the money there is. Take it and go home, that's all. If you like, leave the gun here with me. Here's your money. Yes, *yours*—it *is* yours, if you've got to take a gun out to get it! I know how you feel because I've felt the same way. We've all felt the same way. The graveyards and penitentiaries are full of good American kids who've had bad luck and hard times. They're not criminals. Here," he said gently, "take this money and go home."

The young man brought the gun out of his pocket and pushed it across the counter to Spangler, who dropped it into the cash drawer.

"I don't know who you are," he said, "but no one has ever talked to me the way you have. I don't want the gun, and I won't take the money, and I *am* going home. I bummed my way out here, and I'll bum my way back." He coughed a moment and then said, "I don't know where my mother got the thirty dollars. I know she has no money to spare. I spent some of the money drinking. I gambled some, and—"

"Come on in and sit down," Spangler said. After a moment the young man went to the chair beside Spangler's desk. Spangler sat down on the desk. "What's the matter?" he said.

"I don't know exactly," the young man said. "Maybe T.B. I'm not sure. If I haven't got it, I guess I *ought* to have it, the way I've been living. I don't like to complain. I've had a lot of bad luck, but I know it's my own fault. I'll go now. Thanks a lot—I'll try to remember you some day." The young man turned to leave the office.

"Wait a minute," Spangler said. "Sit down. Take it easy. You've got a lot of time—*now*. You're not rushing things any more. From now on, move a little slower. What's a fellow like you interested in?"

"I don't know. I don't know which way to go, or what to do when I get there, or what to believe, or anything. My father was a preacher, but he's been dead since I was three years old. I just don't know what to do." He looked at Spangler. "What *is* there to do?"

"Nothing in *particular*. Anything. It doesn't matter what a man does. Any good honest work."

"I've always been restless and dissatisfied. I don't know what it is. Nothing means anything to me. I don't like people. I don't like being near them. I don't trust them. I don't like the way they live or talk or the things they believe, or the way they push each other around."

"Every man in the world feels that way at one time or another."

"It's not that I don't understand *myself*. I guess I do. I've got no alibis. I'm responsible for everything. Now, I'm just tired and fed-up and sick. Nothing interests me. The whole world's gone crazy. I can't live the kind of life I want to live and I don't feel like living any other kind. It's not money that I want or need. I know I could get a job, especially now. But I don't like the people you've got to get a job from. They're no good. I don't like being humble to them, and I can't let anybody push me around. I tried to hold a few jobs in York, Pennsylvania. I always had a fight and got fired. Three or four days, a week, or a week and a half. The longest I ever held a job was one month.

"I tried to enlist in the Army in York because I thought that might be a good thing to do—go somewhere—get killed maybe. If they boss you in the Army at least it's for something that's supposed to be halfway decent. I don't know whether it really *is* or not, but at least it's supposed to be. They turned me down. I couldn't pass the physical. It wasn't my lungs alone—it was other things, too. I didn't bother to find out." The young man began to cough again, but this time he coughed for almost a full minute. Spangler brought a small bottle out of the desk drawer.

"Here, take a drink of this."

"Thanks," the young man said. "I drink a little too much, but I *need* a drink now." He took a swallow from the bottle, then handed it back to Spangler. "Thanks," he said again.

Spangler decided he ought to urge the young man to go on talking. "What do you read?" he said.

"Oh, everything. At least I used to when I was home. My father had a lot of books—not religious books only—good books—by good writers. My favorite was William Blake. Maybe you know his stuff. I read every book my father had—some of them twice, a few three times. I used to like to read, but no more. Now I don't even want to look at newspapers. I *know* the news. Corruption and murder all over the place, every day, and not one man in the world able to do anything about it." He held his head in his hands and, speaking softly, he went on without looking up. "I can't thank you for what you've done and for the kind of human being you are, but I must tell you I would have shot you if you had been afraid of me, or unkind. Everybody in the world is afraid or unkind. I know now that I didn't come here with a gun for *money*. I don't know whether you will understand, but I came here with a gun to find out once and for all if the only man in the world I have ever known who has been decent to another man just to be decent—just for itself—was *truly* so. I came to find out if it wasn't an accident. I couldn't believe anybody could be really decent, because it made my whole feeling about everything and everybody untrue—the feeling I have had for a long time that the human race is hopeless and corrupt, that there isn't one man in the world worthy of another man's respect. For a long time I've had contempt for the pathetic as well as for the proud, and then suddenly thousands of miles from home, in a strange city, I found a man who was decent. It bothered me. It bothered me for a long time. I couldn't believe it. I had to find out. I wanted it to be true. I wanted to believe it, because I've been telling myself for years: 'Let me find one man uncorrupted by the world so that *I* may be uncorrupted, so that I may believe and live.' I wasn't sure the first time we met, but I'm sure now. I want nothing more from you. You've given me everything I want. You can't give me anything more. You understand, I know. When I get up it shall be to say good-by. You needn't worry about me. I'm going home where I belong. I'm not going to die of this sickness. I'm going to live. And now I'm going to know *how* to live." The young man didn't lift his head for a moment. Then, he got up slowly and looked at Spangler. "Thanks a lot," he said.

Spangler watched him walk out of the office. He went to the cash drawer and put the money back where it belonged. He took the young man's revolver and unloaded it. He put the revolver back in the drawer and dropped the shells into his coat pocket. Then he went to the steel rack where each day's telegrams were tied into a bundle. In one bundle he found the telegram the boy had sent his mother. He took a fresh telegraph blank and began to write a telegram:

MRS. MARGARET STRICKMAN
1874 BIDDLE STREET
YORK, PENNSYLVANIA
   DEAR MA: THANKS FOR THE MONEY. WILL BE HOME SOON. EVERYTHING FINE.

He read the words of the message and then decided to change "fine" to "O.K." Then he remembered the young man a moment and added, "Love, John." He went to Mr. Grogan's place at the telegraph table and called for an operator. His call was answered after several moments and then Spangler tapped out the telegram, after which he talked to the operator at the other end, smiling as he listened to the dots and dashes and made his answers. When he was through talking he got up and went to his own desk.

Mr. Grogan came in and sat in the chair where the young man had been sitting.

"How do you feel now?" Spangler said.

"Better, of course," Mr. Grogan said. "I had *two* drinks, Tom. I listened to the soldiers singing. They love that pianola and those old songs—songs they never heard before."

"You do love me, don't you?" Spangler said. "That's what she says, all the time, and that's the way she says it. I believe I'm going to marry her."

Spangler stopped dreaming of Diana Steed a moment to study the face of his old friend. "The old songs are O.K."

"Tom," Mr. Grogan said, "remember the way old Davenport used to sing those ballads?"

"Sure," Spangler said, "as long as this office is here I'll hear him. I can hear him now. But not old ballads only—church songs, too. Don't forget the church songs old Davenport used to sing every Sunday."

"I haven't forgotten them. I remember every one of them. Of course he liked to pretend he was an atheist, but all day Sunday he sang hymns—chewing tobacco, sending telegrams, singing, and squirting tobacco juice out of his mouth into the spittoon. First thing in the morning he'd start out with 'Welcome, delightful morn, thou day of sacred rest.' He was a great man, Tom. Then he'd holler out, 'This is the day of light. Let there be light today.'"

"I remember," Spangler said.

"Then, he would sing, 'Lord, God of morning and of night, We thank Thee for Thy gift of light.' The great unbeliever—and more than anything he loved light and life. And then at the end of the day he would get up from his chair slowly, stretch himself and sing very softly, 'Now the day is over, night is drawing nigh.' He knew all of the good old songs, and he loved every one of them. 'Saviour,' he would shout, pretending to be an atheist who was mocking, 'Saviour, breathe an evening blessing, Ere repose our spirits seal; Sin and want we come confessing, Thou canst save and Thou canst heal.' "

The telegraph operator became silent to remember his old friend who had been dead these many long years. "It's the truth, Tom. What he sang is the truth."

The manager of the telegraph office smiled at his old friend and patted him on the shoulder as he moved to turn off the lights and close the office for the night.

23. The Nightmare

HOMER MACAULEY was in bed at last, tossing and turning. He dreamed he was running the two-twenty low hurdles again, but every time he got to a hurdle, Byfield was there to stop him. He hurdled anyway and they went down. At every hurdle Byfield was there. Finally the injury to Homer's leg was so painful that when he tried to run, he fell. He got up and pasted Byfield in the mouth. He shouted at the man, "You can't stop me! You can never stop me—low hurdles, high hurdles, any kind of hurdles!"

He began to run again, limping at first but soon running

well, but the next hurdle was inhumanly high—eight feet
—nevertheless, Homer Macauley, perhaps the greatest
man in Ithaca, California, went over the hurdle with perfect form.

Next in the dream he was in his uniform riding his bicycle swiftly down a narrow street. Suddenly Byfield stood in
the way. But Homer pushed toward the man more swiftly
than ever. "I told you—you can't stop me!" He lifted upward on the handlebars, and the bicycle began to rise and
fly. It flew directly over Byfield's head and came down
lightly on the other side of him. But just as it reached the
pavement, Byfield stood in the way again! Again the bicycle left the street and flew over the man. But this time it
stayed aloft, suspended twenty feet over Byfield's head.
The man stood in the street, amazed and displeased. "You
can't do that!" he shouted. "You're breaking the law of
gravity."

"What do I care about the law of gravity?" Homer
shouted at the man in the street. "Or the law of averages,
or the law of supply and demand, or any other law? *You
can't stop me!* Worm, rust and rot—I have no time for
you." The messenger rode on through space, leaving the
ugly man alone in the street, as inferior as any inferiority
could ever be.

Now Homer flew high, among dark clouds. As the messenger rode through the sky, he watched another bicycle
rider in a messenger's uniform very much like his own but
moving even faster than himself, push out of black cloud.
The second messenger, strangely, seemed to be Homer
himself, but at the same time he seemed to be someone
Homer feared. Homer raced after the second messenger to
find out who he really was.

The two riders raced a good long distance before Homer
began to catch up. Suddenly the other messenger turned,
and Homer was amazed that the messenger looked exactly
like himself, but at the same time was unmistakably—not
so much in appearance as in feeling—the messenger of
Death. The riders were swiftly coming to Ithaca. Homer
raced after the messenger of Death, moving swifter than
ever before. Far down in the distance he could see the

lonely lights of the town and the lonely streets and houses. Homer was determined to head off the other messenger, to keep him away from Ithaca. Nothing in the world was more important than to keep this messenger from reaching Ithaca.

The two riders raced hard and decently, with no tricks of any kind. They were both tiring now, but at last Homer was alongside the other rider, and was heading him away from Ithaca. Then, with a sudden burst of speed, the other messenger drew away and turned back toward the little town. Deeply disappointed in himself but still racing with all his might, Homer watched the other messenger ride on toward Ithaca, leaving Homer far behind. Now Homer could race no longer. There was no energy left with which to chase the messenger of Death. The boy almost collapsed on his bicycle, which began to fall, and Homer began to cry out to the other messenger, "Don't go to Ithaca! Leave them alone!"

The boy sobbed with terrible grief.

In the house on Santa Clara Avenue the dreamer's little brother Ulysses stood beside Homer and listened. He went through the dark house to his mother's bed and shook her. When she sat up, he took her hand and without a word they went to Homer's bed. Mrs. Macauley listened to her son a moment, then put Ulysses back in his bed, tucked him in, and sat down beside the weeping boy. She spoke to him very softly.

"Be still now, Homer. Rest now. You are very tired. You must rest. Sleep now. Sleep peacefully." The messenger began to stop sobbing and soon his troubled expression went away. "Sleep now," his mother said. "Sleep peacefully."

The boy began to sleep. The mother looked over at her youngest son and he, too, was now asleep. In the corner of the room she thought she saw Matthew Macauley standing and watching, smiling. She got up quietly, took the alarm clock, and went back to her own room.

The messenger's sleep moved from the realm of black terror to the realm of light and peace. Homer Macauley, in this new sleep, found himself lying on his back under a fig tree beside a brook. "This," he said to himself, "would be up by Riverview where I saw the fig tree by the lazy stream, under the sun that burned with a kind of laughter that made everything else laugh. I remember this place. It was last summer and Marcus and I came here to swim, and then we sat on the bank of the river and talked about what we would do in the world." And now, knowing the pleasantness of the place he had reached and feeling the warmth of his memory of it, he stretched out comfortably on the grass under the tree—and forgot completely that he was asleep.

He was in the same old clothes he wore that summer day with Marcus. Before him, stuck into the soft earth, he saw the fishing pole, but this was not from that summer day—this was from a long, long time ago. Now, far away through the wilderness of grass and bough Homer Macauley beheld the beautiful Helen Eliot, barefoot like himself, and in a plain gingham dress, walking over a narrow path toward him. "That's Helen Eliot," Homer said to himself. "That's the girl I love." He sat up smiling, watched her walk, and then got to his feet and went to greet her. Without a word and with something like solemnity, Homer took the girl's hand and together they walked to the fig tree. There he removed his shirt and pants, and dived into the sweet water. The girl went behind a shrub and there she removed her dress. Homer watched her come to the riverbank, stand a moment, and then dive. They swam around in the gently flowing water, and then they left it together to lie on the sand in the sun, and sleep.

24. The Apricot Tree

ULYSSES MACAULEY was up very early, skipping through the morning's first light to the yard of a man who owned a cow. When he reached the yard, Ulysses saw the cow. The small boy stood and watched the cow a long time. At last the man who owned the cow came out of the small house. He was carrying a bucket and a stool. The man went straight to the cow and began to milk. Ulysses moved in closer until finally he was directly behind the man. Still, he couldn't see enough, so he knelt down, almost under the cow. The man saw the boy but did not say anything. He

went right on milking. The cow, however, turned and
looked at Ulysses. Ulysses looked back at the cow. It
seemed perhaps that the cow did not like to have the boy
so close. Ulysses got out from under the cow, walked
away, and watched from near by. The cow, in turn,
watched Ulysses, so that the small boy believed they might
become friends.

On his way home, Ulysses stopped to watch a man who
was building a barn. The man was high-strung, nervous,
impatient, and should never have undertaken the work. He
labored furiously, making all kinds of mistakes, while
Ulysses watched and tried unsuccessfully to understand.

Ulysses got back to Santa Clara Avenue just in time to
see Mr. Arena go off to work on his bicycle. Mary Arena
waved to her father from the porch and then went back
into the house.

It was Saturday morning in Ithaca. Out of a house not
far away came a boy of eight or nine. Ulysses waved, and
the boy waved back. This boy was Lionel Cabot, the neighborhood simpleton, but all the same a great human being,
faithful, generous and sweet-tempered. After a moment
Lionel looked over at Ulysses again, and, for want of
something better to do, waved again. Ulysses waved back.
This continued at frequent intervals until August Gottlieb
came out of his house next door to Ara's Market.

Auggie had been the leader of the neighborhood boys
since Homer Macauley had retired from that position at
the age of twelve. The new leader looked around for his
followers. He rejected Lionel as too dumb and Ulysses as
too little, but waved a greeting to each of them nevertheless. He then went out to the middle of the street and whistled, newsboy style. It was a loud whistle, authoritative,
commanding, and absolutely final. Auggie waited with the
confidence of a man who knows what he is doing and what
results he is going to get. Immediately windows were
opened and replies were whistled. Soon a number of boys
came running to the corner. In less than three minutes the
gang was together—Auggie Gottlieb, the leader, Nickie
Paloota, Alf Rife, and Shag Manoogian.

"Where we going, Auggie?" Nickie said.

"To see if Henderson's apricots are ripe."

"Can I come?" Lionel said.

"O.K., Lionel. If they're ripe, will you steal some?"

"It's a sin to steal," Lionel said.

"Not apricots," Augie said, making an important distinction. "Ulysses," he said, "you go home. This is not for little boys. It's dangerous."

Ulysses moved away three steps, stopped and watched. He wasn't hurt or offended by Auggie's orders. He understood the code. He was just not old enough yet, that's all. But while he respected the law, he couldn't resist wanting to be in the gang anyhow.

The boys started off for Henderson's. Instead of going by way of streets and sidewalks, they took alleys, crossed empty lots, and climbed over fences. They wanted to get there the hard way, the adventurous way. Not far behind, at a safe distance, Ulysses followed.

"Ripe apricots are just about the best-tasting fruit in the world," Auggie said to the members of the gang.

"Do apricots get ripe in March?" Nickie Paloota said.

"It's almost April," Auggie said. *"Early* apricots get ripe in no time if the sun shines a lot."

"It's been raining lately, though," Alf Rife said.

"Where do you think apricots get their juice from?" Auggie said. "From rain. Rain is just as important as sunshine to apricots."

"Sunshine in the daytime, rain at night," Shag Manoogian said. "Warm them up, give them water. I'll bet there's a lot of ripe apricots on the tree."

"Boy, I hope so," Alf Rife said.

"It's too early for apricots," Nickie Paloota said. "They weren't ripe last year until June."

"That was last year," Auggie said. "This is this year."

From a distance of about one hundred yards the boys stopped to admire the famous apricot tree—all green and pretty, very old and very big. It stood in the corner of Henderson's backyard. For ten years the boys of the neighborhood had raided old man Henderson's apricot tree. In the broken-down house every spring Mr. Henderson had watched their coming with fascination and delight—always satisfying the boys by appearing at the last minute and scaring them away. Now, in the house at a curtained window, he looked up from his book.

"Well, look at that!" he said to himself. "Coming to steal apricots in March, in the dead of Winter." He peeked out at the boys again, whispering as if he were one of them. "Coming to get apricots off old man Henderson's tree. Here they come. Slowly, now. Hah-hah," he laughed, "look at them! And look at that little one! Surely not more than four years old. He's a new one. Come on, boys. Come to the wonderful old tree. If I could ripen them for you to steal, I'd do it—"

He watched the boys as Auggie instructed, directed, and led the attack. The boys surrounded the tree cautiously, with a mingling in their hearts of hope and fear. Even if the apricots were green, they were on Henderson's tree and belonged to him, and therefore their coming for the apricots was the same as if the apricots were ripe—therefore they *hoped* the apricots *were* ripe. But they were afraid, too. They were afraid of Henderson, they were afraid of sin, of capture and guilt, and they were afraid the apricots weren't ripe yet.

"Maybe he ain't home," Nickie Paloota whispered as the boys almost reached the tree.

"He's home," Auggie said. "He's *always* home. He's hiding, that's all. It's a trap. He wants to catch us. Careful, everybody. There's no telling where he'll be. Ulysses, you go home."

Obediently Ulysses retreated three steps and stopped to watch the magnificent duel with the magnificent tree.

"Are they ripe?" Shag said. "Do you see any color, Auggie?"

"Only green," Auggie said. "That's leaves. The apricots are underneath. Easy now, everybody. Where's Lionel?"

"Here I am," Lionel whispered. He was terribly afraid.

"Well," Auggie said, "be on your toes. If you see old man Henderson, run!"

"Where is he?" Lionel said as if Henderson might be invisible or no bigger than a rabbit, something likely to jump up suddenly out of the grass.

"What do you mean where is he? He's in the house, I guess. But you can never tell about Henderson. He might be hiding outside some place, waiting to take us by surprise."

"Are you going to climb the tree?" Alf Rife said.

"Who else?" Auggie said. "But let's see if the apricots are ripe first."

"Ripe or green," Shag Manoogian said, "we want to steal at least *some* of them, Auggie."

"Don't worry. We will. If they're ripe, we'll steal a *lot* of them."

"What are you going to say at Sunday School tomorrow?" Lionel said.

"Stealing apricots isn't stealing, like stealing in the Bible, Lionel. This is different."

"Then, what are you scared of?"

"Who's scared? We've just got to be careful, that's all. What's the use of getting caught if you can get away?"

"I don't see any ripe apricots," Lionel said.

"You see a tree, don't you?" Auggie said.

"I see a tree, all right. That's *all*, though—just a big tree —all green. It sure is pretty, too, Auggie."

Now, the gang was almost under the tree. Ulysses followed not far behind. He was absolutely unafraid. He didn't understand at all, but he was sure this was very important stuff—something about trees, something about apricots. The boys studied the branches of the old apricot tree, green with fine young leaf. The apricots were all very small, very green, and obviously very hard.

"Not ripe yet," Alf Rife said.

"Yeah," Auggie admitted. "I guess they need a couple more days. Maybe next Saturday."

"Next Saturday—*sure*," Shag said.

"There's a *lot* of them, though," Auggie said.

"We can't go back empty-handed," Shag said. "We've got to get at least *one* of them—green or ripe—*one* of them, anyway."

"O.K.," Auggie said. "I'll get it. Now, the rest of you be ready to run." Auggie dashed to the tree, swung up into it on one of its lower branches while the gang and Mr. Henderson and Ulysses watched with fascination, amazement, and admiration. Then, Mr. Henderson stepped out of the house onto the back-porch steps. All the boys went off like a school of startled minnows.

"Auggie!" Shag Manoogian shouted. *"Henderson!"*

Like a frightened orang-outang in the jungle, Auggie bounced around in the tree, hung from a branch, and then dropped to the ground. He was running almost before his feet touched the ground, but he noticed Ulysses and stopped suddenly, shouting at the boy, *"Run,* Ulysses! Run —*run!"*

Ulysses, however, didn't budge. He couldn't figure it out. Auggie rushed back to the small boy, lifted him off his feet, and ran with him while Henderson watched. When all the boys had disappeared and everything was quiet again, the old man smiled and looked up into the tree. Then he turned around and went back into the house.

25. Mr. Ara

ONE BY ONE the members of August Gottlieb's Secret Society returned from their escape from old man Henderson and gathered in front of Ara's Market to wait there for the arrival of their leader. At last the great man was observed by his devoted followers coming around the alley holding the hand of Ulysses Macauley. The members of the Society waited silently for the arrival of the leader, who was soon among them. The face of the leader was searched by each of the followers and then the one named Alf Rife said, "Did you get an apricot, Auggie?"

The leader looked at this faithless one and said, "You don't have to ask that. You saw me in the tree. You *know* I got an apricot."

Now, all the members spoke in one voice. (All, that is, excepting Lionel, who was not really a member at all.) They said with great admiration, "Let's see it, Auggie. Let's see the apricot."

The little boy Ulysses watched everything, still completely unsure of the mysterious values involved but still certain that whatever these values might be they were surely of greater importance than anything else in the world—at that moment, at any rate.

"Let's see the apricot you stole, Auggie," the members of the Society said again. "Come on, let's see it."

August Gottlieb quietly fished into the pocket of his overalls and brought out a clenched fist which he thrust before him. His followers gathered around and looked directly upon the fist. When everyone was appropriately quiet and respectful, August Gottlieb opened his fist.

There in the palm of his hand was a small green apricot the size of a quail egg.

The followers of the great religious leader smiled at the miraculous object in the palm of his hand, and Lionel—the kindest of them all, even though he was not a bona-fide member of the religious sect—lifted Ulysses so that he too could see the small green object. Having seen the green apricot, Ulysses squirmed, got down, and then ran for home, not disappointed, only eager to tell someone.

Now, out of his store, stepped Ara himself, the man who had established Ara's Market in this neighborhood of Ithaca, California, seven years ago. He was a tall, lean-faced, melancholy yet comical man who wore a white grocer's apron over his plain business suit. He stood a moment on the small porch of the store to look down at the new Messiah and his disciples and to listen to their delighted expressions of adoration for the Holy Image.

"Auggie, you!" he said. "You, Shag! Nickie! Alfo, you! Lionel, you!—what you call this? United States Congress Washington? Go some odder place hold important meeting. This market, not Congress."

"Oh, sure, Mr. Ara," August Gottlieb said. "We'll go across the street to the empty lot. Do you want to see an apricot?"

"You got apricot?" the grocer said. "Where you get apricot?"

"Off a tree. Want to see it?"

"Is not apricot now. Apricot come in two more month. In Maytime."

"This is a March apricot," the leader of the whirling-dervishes said to the grocer. Again he opened his fist, revealing the small hard green object. "Look at it, Mr. Ara," Auggie said, and then paused. "Pretty?"

"All right, all right," Mr. Ara said. "Pretty. Very fine apricot. Now, go hold meeting United States Congress Washington some odder place. Today Saturday. Market open for business. Don't crowd small store first thing in morning. Give chance. Small store get scared, run away."

"O.K., Mr. Ara," Auggie said, "we won't crowd your store. We'll go across the street now. Come on, you guys."

Mr. Ara watched the small migration of the religious fanatics. He was about to go back into the store when a small boy who resembled him came out of the store and stood beside him.

"Papa?"

"Hah, John?"

"Give me apple," the boy said to the man. He spoke earnestly, almost sadly.

The father took the son by the hand and together they went into the store to the counter where the fresh fruit was stacked in piles.

"Apple?" the father said to the boy. He took an apple from the pile—the very best apple in the pile—and handed it to the boy. "All right, apple."

The father went behind the counter of his store to wait for a customer, and in the meantime to look upon his son, surely as melancholy as himself, even though there was a difference of at least forty years in their ages. The son took one enormous bite out of the apple, chewed it slowly, swallowed it, and then for a moment seemed to think about it, while the father himself thought about it, too. The apple

did not make the boy happy. He put it down on the counter
in front of his father and then looked up at the man. There
they were, in Ithaca, California, probably seven thousand
miles from what had been for centuries their home in the
world. Naturally there was a loneliness in each of them,
but no one could know for sure that the same loneliness
might not be in them had they been seven thousand miles
away, back home. There on the floor of his store stood the
father's son, and the father looked at the son—at his own
face in the boy, his own eyes, and beyond the eyes surely
his own character. There was the same man, only younger.
The father took the rejected apple, attacked it with an enormous crackling bite, and stood chewing and swallowing.
He might have been tragic Lear himself, judging from the
swiftness and noisiness of his stentorian chewing. An apple
was too good a thing in the world to be wasted, and therefore if his son would not eat it, then he must eat it, even
though he had no passion for apples or for their flavor. He
simply knew that it was wrong to waste anything. He continued to bite into the apple, to chew, and to swallow, as if
in dramatic soliloquy. At last, however, it was a little too
much—there was a little too much apple. It would be necessary to waste *some* of it. With recklessness and perhaps a
small amount of regret, he flung the remains of the apple
into the garbage can.

Now, the son spoke again. "Papa?"

"Hah, John?"

"Give me orange."

The father selected the biggest orange in the neat pile of
oranges and handed it to the boy. "Orange? All right   orange."

The boy bit into the peel of the orange, then began to
finish the job of peeling with his fingers, working slowly
but efficiently at first but after a moment accelerating his
effort with such an intensity that even the father began to
feel, as surely the son felt, that beneath the peeling of this
growth of tree would be not simply the flesh of an orange
but the heart's final fulfillment. The boy placed the peel-
ings of the orange on the counter in front of the man,
broke the orange in half, peeled off one section, put it in

his mouth, chewed and swallowed. But alas, no. It was truly an orange, but it was truly *not* the heart's final fulfillment. The son waited a moment, then put the rest of the orange in front of his father. Again the father took up the unfinished work and silently began trying to finish it. But soon the limit was reached, and a little less than half of the orange went into the garbage can.

"Papa?" the boy said after a moment, and again the father replied, "Hah, John?"

"Give me candy."

"Candy? All right—candy."

From the candy showcase the father selected the most popular five-cent bar of candy and handed it to the boy. The boy studied this manufactured substance, removed the wax paper, and took a big bite out of the chocolate-covered candy and again slowly chewed and swallowed. But again it was nothing—only candy—sweet, yes; otherwise, nothing, truly nothing. Once again the son returned to the father another substance of the world which had failed to bring him completion. Patiently the father accepted the responsibility—to avoid waste. He picked up the candy bar, started to bite into it and then changed his mind. He turned and flung the candy into the garbage can. He felt bitterly angry, and in his heart he cursed some people seven thousand miles away who had once seemed to him to be inhuman, or at least ignorant. *Those dogs!* he said.

"Papa?"

"Hah, John?"

"Give me banana."

The father sighed this time but did not abandon all faith. "Banana? All right—banana." He examined the bunch of bananas hanging over the piles of fruit and finally discovered what he believed to be the ripest and the sweetest banana of the bunch. He plucked this banana off the bunch and handed it to the boy.

At last a customer came into the store. The customer was a man Mr. Ara had never before seen. The storekeeper and the customer nodded to one another in greeting, and then the man said with an accent all his own, "You got cookies?"

"Cook-ies?" the grocer said eagerly. "What kind cook-ies you want?"

Another customer came into the store. This customer was Ulysses Macauley. He stood to one side, listening and watching, waiting his turn.

"You got cookies, raisins in?" the man said to the grocer.

"Cook-ies, raisins in?" the grocer said. This was a problem. "Cook-ies, raisins in," he said again, almost whispering. "Cook-ies, raisins in," he said still again. The grocer looked around the store. The grocer's son put the banana on the counter in front of his father—rejected.

"Papa?"

The father looked at the boy and then spoke very swiftly. "You want apple, I give you apple. You want orange, I give you orange. You want candy, I give you candy. You want banana, I give you banana. What you want *now?*"

"Cookies," the boy said.

"What kind cook-ies you want?" the father said to the boy, not forgetting the customer, and in fact, speaking *to* the customer, but at the same time speaking to his son, and at the same time speaking to everybody, everywhere—everybody wanting things.

"Cookies, raisins in," the boy said.

With furious restraint the father almost whispered his reply to his son, but instead of looking at his son he looked at the customer. "I got no cook-ies," he whispered. *"No* kind cook-ies. Why you want cook-ies? I got everything, but no cook-ies. What's cook-ies? What you want?"

"Cookies," the man said patiently, "for small boy."

"I got no cook-ies," the grocer said again. "I got small boy too." The grocer pointed to his own son. "I give him apple, orange, candy, banana, lots of good things." He looked the customer straight in the eye, and almost as if he were angry, he said, again, "What you *want?*"

"My broder's boy," the customer said. "He's got influenza. He cry—he want cookies. 'Cookies, raisins in,' he say."

But every man lives his own life and every life has its

own theme, so that again the grocer's son looked at his father and said, "Papa?"

But now the father refused to look at the boy. Instead, he looked at the man whose nephew was ill and wanted cookies with raisins in them. He looked at the man with understanding, with sympathy, and yet with a kind of peasant rage, not against the man but against the world itself, against illness, against pain, against loneliness, against the heart wanting what it can never have. The grocer was angry at himself too because even though he had established this market in Ithaca, California, seven thousand miles from home, he did not have cookies with raisins in them, he did not have that which the sick boy wanted. The grocer pointed at his son and spoke to the man.

"Apple," the grocer said, "orange, candy, banana—no cookies. He's my boy. Three years old. Not sick. He want many things. I don't *know* what he want. Nobody know what he want. He just want. He look at God. He say, Give me dis, give me dat—but he never satisfied. Always he want. Always he feel bad. Poor God has got nothing for such sadness. He give everything — world — sunshine — moder — fader — broder — sister — onkle — cousin — house, farm, stove, table, bed—poor God give everything—but nobody happy—everybody like small boy sick with influenza—everybody say give me cookies—raisins in." The grocer stopped a moment to take a very deep breath. When he exhaled he said very loudly to the customer, *"Is no cookies—raisins in."*

The grocer began to move with an impatience and a fury which were almost majestic. First he took a paper bag and snapped it open. Then he began to toss things into the bag. "Here's orange, very pretty. Here's apple. Wonderful. Here's banana. Taste very good." Now, gently, and with great courtesy and sincere sympathy for the man and for the man's sick nephew, the grocer handed the bag to the customer. "Take to little boy. No pay. I no want money." And then again he said very softly, "Is no cookies, raisins in."

"He cry," the man said. "He feel very bad. He say, 'Cookies, raisins in.' Thank you very much, but we already

give small boy apple, orange, odder things." The man put
the bag down on the counter. "Sick boy say, 'Give me
cookies, raisins in.' Apple, orange—no good. Excuse me, I
go try chain store. Maybe *they* got cookies, raisins in."

"All right, my friend," the grocer whispered. "You go
try chain store—but they no got cookies, raisins in. Nobody got."

Almost shyly the stranger left the store. For a full
minute the grocer stood behind the counter staring at his
son. Suddenly he began to speak in his own language, Armenian.

"The world's gone mad," he said. "In Russia alone, so
near our own country, our own beautiful little nation, millions of people, millions of children, every day go hungry.
They are cold, pathetic, barefooted— They walk around—
no place to sleep—they pray for a piece of dry bread—
somewhere to lie down and rest—one night of peaceful
sleep. And what about us? What do we do? Here we are in
Ithaca, California, in this great country, America. What do
we do? We wear good clothes. We put on good shoes every
morning when we get up from sleep. We walk around with
no one in the streets to come with guns or to burn our
houses or to murder our children or brothers or fathers.
We take rides out into the country in automobiles. We eat
the best food. Every night when we go to bed we sleep—
and then what are we? We are discontented. We are *still*
discontented." The grocer shouted this amazing truth at his
little son with terrible love for the boy. "Apple," he said,
"orange, candy, banana, for God's sake, little fellow, don't
do this! If I do it, you are my son, better than me, and
therefore you must not do this. Be happy! Be happy! I am
unhappy, but *you* must be happy." He pointed to the back
door of the store which led into the house, and obediently,
very sober-faced, the little boy left the store and entered
the house.

Now the grocer spent a moment trying to compose himself. At last he believed he was calm enough to speak
quietly to the customer in the store, Ulysses Macauley. He
turned to the boy and tried to be cheerful. He even smiled.
"What you want, little boy Ulysses?"

"Mush."

"What kind mush you want?"

"H-O."

"Two kinds H-O, little boy Ulysses. "Regular kind, and quick-cooking kind. Two kinds. Slow, quick. Old, new. What kind your mama want, little boy Ulysses?"

Ulysses thought about this a moment and then said, "H-O."

"Old kind or new kind?"

But the little boy didn't know, so the grocer decided for him. "All right, new kind, modern. Eighteen cents, please, little boy Ulysses."

Ulysses opened his fist and thrust his arm out toward the grocer, who took the quarter from the boy's hand. The grocer handed Ulysses the change, saying, "Eighteen cents, ninetcen, twenty, and nickel—twenty-five. Thank you, little boy Ulysses."

"You're welcome, Mr. Ara," Ulysses said. He took the package of oatmeal and walked out of the store. It was very difficult to understand anything. First it was apricots on a tree, then it was cookies with raisins in, and then it was the grocer talking to his son in a strange tongue—but even so it was exciting. In the street the little boy kicked up his heel as he did whenever he was pleased, and began to run home.

26. Mrs. Macauley

MRS. MACAULEY had the kitchen table set for one, waiting for her son Homer to come to breakfast. She was setting down a bowl of oatmeal when he came into the kitchen. Her glance at him was only fleeting but even so she knew that the strange experience of his dream last night was still upon him. Even though he himself perhaps did not know he had wept in his sleep, his spirit seemed hushed as the spirit of a man is hushed after grief. Even his voice seemed deeper and gentler.

"I didn't want to sleep this late," he said. "It's almost nine-thirty. What happened to the alarm clock?"

"You're working hard," Mrs. Macauley said. "You must rest, too."

"I'm not working so hard. Besides, tomorrow's Sunday." He said his morning prayer, only it seemed to last twice as long as usual. Then he picked up his spoon and was about to begin to eat when he stopped and studied the spoon strangely. He looked toward his mother who was busy at the kitchen sink. "Ma?"

"Yes, Homer?"

"I didn't talk to you last night when I came home, because it was like you said. I *couldn't* talk. All of a sudden on the way home last night I started to cry. You know I never did cry when I was little or at school when I was in trouble. I always felt ashamed to cry. Even Ulysses never cries. But last night I just couldn't help it, and I don't remember if I was ashamed, even. I don't think I was. And I couldn't come straight home, either. I rode out to Ithaca Wine and then I rode across town to the high school. On the way there I rode past a house where some people had been having a party earlier in the evening—the house was dark now. I took those people a telegram. You know the kind of telegram it was. Then, I went back to town and rode all around the streets looking at everything—all the buildings, all the places I've known all my life, all of them full of people. And then at last I really *saw* Ithaca and I really knew the people who live in Ithaca. I felt sorry for all of them and I even prayed that nothing would happen to them. After that I stopped crying. I thought a fellow would never cry when he got to be grown up, but it seems as if that's when a fellow *starts*, because that's when a fellow starts finding out about things." He stopped a moment, and then his voice became even more somber than it had been. "Almost everything a man finds out is bad or sad." He waited a moment for some word from his mother but she didn't speak and didn't turn away from her work. "Why is that so?" he said.

Mrs. Macauley began to speak, still turned away from him. "You'll find out. No one can tell you. Each man finds out for himself, in his own way, because each man *is* the world."

"Why did I cry, and after I stopped crying why couldn't I talk? Why was there nothing for me to say—to anybody? To you, or to myself?"

"Pity—I suppose it was pity that made you cry. Unless a man has pity he is not truly a man. If a man has not wept at the world's pain he is only half a man, and there will always be pain in the world. Knowing this does not mean that a man shall despair. A good man will seek to take pain out of things. A foolish man will not even notice it, except in himself. And the poor unfortunate evil man will drive pain deeper into things and spread it about wherever he goes. But each man is guiltless, I'm afraid, for he did not ask to come here and did not come brandnew, from nowhere and nothing. He came from people. I really don't believe the evil know they *are* evil. It's just their bad luck, that's all. Eat your breakfast like a sensible fellow."

Suddenly he felt it was all right to eat.

27. Lionel

ULYSSES MACAULEY and his best friend Lionel Cabot—the *great* Lionel—came into the Macauley kitchen. There was no mistaking this friendship, even though Lionel was a good six years older than Ulysses. They walked together and stood about together as only the very best of friends do, easily and with scarcely any need for one or the other to speak.

"Mrs. Macauley," Lionel said. "I came to ask permission —can Ulysses go to the pubalic liberry with me? I got to take back a book for my sister Lillian."

"All right, Lionel," Mrs. Macauley said. "But why aren't you with the others—Auggie and Alf and Shag and the other boys?"

"They—" Lionel began to say and then stopped, from embarrassment. After a moment he began again. "They chased me away. They don't like me because I'm dumb."

"You're no such thing, Lionel," Mrs. Macauley said. "You're the nicest boy in this neighborhood. But don't you be angry at the other boys, because they're all nice boys, too."

"I'm not angry," Lionel said. "I like every one of them. But every time I make a little mistake in a game they chase me away. They even swear at me. Every little mistake I make they get sore at me. 'That's all, Lionel,' they say. And when they say it, I know I've got to go. Sometimes I don't even last five minutes. Sometimes I make a mistake the first thing I do. And then they say, 'That's all, Lionel.' I don't even know what mistake I made. What do they want me to do? That's all I want to know, but nobody will tell me. Every Saturday they chase me away. Ulysses is the only one who sticks with me. He's the only partner I've got. But some day the others are going to be sorry. When the time comes and the others come to me and want me to help them—well, Mrs. Macauley, I'm going to help them, and then they're going to be sorry they chased me away all the time. Can I have a drink of water?"

"Of course, Lionel." Mrs. Macauley filled a glass of water for the boy, and he drank it all quickly, making the kind of sound that boys make when water is still the most wonderful drink in the world.

"Don't you want a drink of water, too, Ulysses?" Lionel said.

Ulysses indicated by nodding that he would like a glass of water, too. After Ulysses had swallowed the water, Lionel said, "Well, I guess we'll go to the pubalic liberry now, Mrs. Macauley." The two friends walked out of the house.

When the two boys were gone, Homer said, "Was Marcus like Ulysses when he was little?"

"How do you mean?"

"You know, the way Ulysses is—interested in everything, always watching. Doesn't ever say anything but always gets a kick out of everything. Seems to like everybody and everybody seems to like him. He doesn't know many words. He can't read, but you can almost always understand him by just looking at him. You can almost understand what he's telling you even if he doesn't say a word. Was Marcus like that, too?"

"Well, Marcus and Ulysses *are* brothers, so of course Ulysses is something like Marcus, but they're not *exactly* alike."

"Ulysses is going to be a great man some day, isn't he?"

"Perhaps not in the eyes of the world, but he is going to be great, of course, because he's great now."

"Marcus was great when he was little, too, wasn't he?"

"You've all a lot in common, of course, but not too much. Marcus was not restless, as you are. He was shy and would rather be alone than out looking for people to see, like Ulysses. Marcus liked to read and listen to music and just sit around or go for long walks."

"Well, Ulysses certainly *likes* Marcus."

"Ulysses likes everybody," Mrs. Macauley said. "He likes everybody in the world."

"Sure," Homer said, "but he likes Marcus *especially*, and I know why, too, because Marcus is still a child, even if he is in the Army. I guess a child looks for a child in everyone else he meets. And if he finds a child in somebody grown up, I guess he likes that person more than he likes the others. I wish I could begin to be grown up the way Ulysses is a child. I guess I admire him more than anybody else in the world outside of our family. Did he tell you what happened to him yesterday?"

"He didn't say a word about it. Auggie came and told us."

"Well, what did he say when he came into the house after I brought him home from the telegraph office?"

"He didn't say anything. He just sat down, listened to the music, and then we had supper. When I put him to bed he said, 'Big Chris.' That's all, and went to sleep. I had no idea who Big Chris was until Auggie told me."

"Who is Ulysses like—most of all?"

"Like his father."

"Did you know Papa when he was little?"

"Lord, no!" Mrs. Macauley said. "How could I? Your father was seven years older than me. Ulysses is like your father as your father was *all* his life. Oh, I've had good luck, thank God. My kids are human beings, besides being children. They might have been children only, and then my luck wouldn't have been so good. What's the matter with your leg?"

"Nothing," Homer said. "I took a little spill. I'm going to the telegraph office."

Homer left the house. His mother heard him bounce his bike several times to see if there was enough air in the tires, and then she saw him ride around the house headed for town.

28. At the Public Library

THE GOOD FRIENDS, Lionel and Ulysses, walked to the public library. On their way, a funeral procession emerged from the First Ithaca Presbyterian Church. Pallbearers carried a plain casket to an old Packard hearse. Following the casket the two boys saw a handful of mourners.

"Come on, Ulysses," Lionel said, "it's a funeral!" They ran half a block, Lionel holding Ulysses by the hand, and very soon they were at the center of everything.

"That's the casket," Lionel whispered. "Somebody's dead in there. I wish I knew who it is. See the flowers.

They give them flowers when they die. See them crying. Those are the people who knew him."

Lionel turned to a man who wasn't very busy. The man had just blown his nose and touched his handkerchief to the corners of his eyes.

"Who's dead?" Lionel asked the man.

"It's poor little Johnny Merryweather, the hunchback," the man said.

Lionel turned to Ulysses. "It's poor little Johnny Merryweather, the hunchback."

"Seventy years old," the man said.

"Seventy years old," Lionel said to Ulysses.

"Sold popcorn on the corner of Mariposa and Broadway for thirty years."

"Sold popcorn on the corner of—" Lionel stopped suddenly and looked at the man. He almost shouted. "You mean the popcorn man?"

"Yes, Johnny Merryweather—gone to his rest."

"I knew *him!*" Lionel shouted. "I bought popcorn off of him many times! Did *he* die?"

"Yes, peacefully. In his sleep. Gone to his Maker."

"I know Johnny Merryweather!" Lionel said, almost crying. "I didn't know his name was Johnny Merryweather, but I knew him."

Lionel turned to Ulysses and put his arm around his friend. "It's Johnny," he almost wept. "Johnny Merryweather. One of my best friends, gone to his Maker."

The hearse drove away and very soon there was no one in front of the church except Lionel and Ulysses. Somehow it seemed wrong for Lionel to leave the place where he learned that the man who had died was a man he knew, even though he had never known that the man's name was Johnny Merryweather. At last, however, he decided he couldn't stand in front of the church forever, even if he *had* bought popcorn off of Johnny Merryweather many times—so, thinking of the popcorn, almost tasting it again, he went on down the street with Ulysses.

When the two boys entered the public library, they entered an area of profound and solemn silence, as if the funeral services were still going on. There were old men reading newspapers. There were town philosophers sitting over enormous books. There were high school boys and girls doing research, but everyone was hushed, because they were seeking wisdom. They were in the presence of books. They were trying to find out. Lionel not only whispered, he moved on tiptoe. Lionel whispered because he was under the impression that it was out of respect for books, not consideration for readers. Ulysses followed him, also on tiptoe, and they explored the library, each finding many treasures, Lionel—books, and Ulysses—people. Lionel didn't read books and he hadn't come to the public library to borrow one. He just liked to *see* them—the thousands of them. He pointed out a whole row of shelved books to his friend and then whispered, "All of these— and these. And these. Here's a red one. All these. There's a green one. All these."

Finally Mrs. Gallagher, the old librarian, noticed the two boys and went over to them. *She* didn't whisper, however. She spoke right out, as if she were not in the public library at all. This shocked Lionel and made a few people look up from the pages of their books.

"What are you looking for, boy?" Mrs. Gallagher said.

"Books," Lionel whispered softly.

"What books are you looking for?"

"All of them."

"All of them? What do you mean? You can borrow only four books on one card."

"I don't want to borrow *any* of them."

"Well, what in the world *do* you want with them?"

"I just want to look at them."

"Look at them? That is not what the public library is for. You can look *into* them, you can look *at* the pictures in them, but what in the world do you want to look at the outsides of them for?"

"I like to," Lionel whispered. "Can't I?"

"Well," the librarian said, "there's no law against it." She looked at Ulysses. "And who's this?"

"This here's Ulysses. He can't read."

"Can you?"

"No, but he can't, either. That's why we're friends. He's

the only other man I know who can't read."

The old librarian looked at the two friends. This was something brandnew in all the years of her experience at the public library. "Well," she said at last, "perhaps it's just as well that you *can't* read. *I* can. I've been reading books for the past sixty years, and I can't see as how it's made any great difference. Run along now and look at the books all you like."

"Yes, ma'am," Lionel said.

The two friends moved off into still greater realms of mystery and adventure. Lionel pointed out more books to Ulysses. "These," he said. "And those over there. And these. All books, Ulysses." He stopped a moment to think. "I wonder what they say in all these books." He pointed out a whole vast area of them, five shelves full of them. "All these," he said—"I wonder what they say." Finally he discovered a book that was green, like fresh grass. "And this one, this one is pretty, Ulysses."

A little frightened at what he was doing, Lionel lifted the book out of the shelf, held it in his hands a moment and then opened it. "There, Ulysses! A book! There it is! See? They're saying something in here." Now he pointed to something in the print of the book. "There's an 'A.' That's an 'A' right there. There's another letter of some sort. I don't know which one that is. Every letter's different, and every word's different." He sighed and looked around at all the books. "I don't think I'll ever learn to read, but I sure would like to know what they're saying. Now, here's a picture. Here's a picture of a girl. See her?" He turned many pages of the book and said, "More letters and words, straight through to the end of the book. This is the pubalic liberry, Ulysses. Books all over the place." He looked at the print of the book with a kind of reverence, whispering to himself as if he were trying to read. Then he shook his head. "You can't know what a book says, Ulysses, unless you can read, and I can't read."

He closed the book slowly, put it back in its place, and together the two friends tiptoed out of the library. Outside, Ulysses kicked up his heel because it seemed he had learned something new.

29. At the Parlor Lecture Club

HOMER MACAULEY got off his bicycle in front of the Ithaca
Parlor Lecture Club, a white building which was an archi-
tectural cross between a Colonial house and a New England church. It was now two-thirty and the Saturday afternoon lecture was about to begin. Consequently, many
middle-aged ladies, most of them mothers, were cheerfully
entering the building. The messenger took a telegram out
of his hat and studied it. The telegram was addressed to
Rosalie Simms-Peabody, Ithaca Parlor Lecture Club, Ithaca, California. Deliver in Person.

As the messenger walked into the hall, the President of the Club, a rounded lady in her early fifties, was beginning to introduce the lecturer, who was nowhere to be seen. The President of the Club pounded a small walnut-breaker on the table and the audience in the hall began to quiet down.

"I've got a telegram for Rosalie Simms-Peabody," Homer whispered to a lady. "It's to be delivered to her *personally*."

"Rosalie Simms-*Pibity*," the lady corrected him. "Yes, Rosalie Simms-Pibity is expecting the telegram. You are to deliver it to her on the platform when she appears."

"When is that going to be?"

"In a moment now. Just sit down and wait. When Rosalie Simms-Pibity appears, run right up onto the stage and call out very clearly, 'Telegram for Rosalie Simms-Pibity!' Not *Peabody*, boy."

"Yes, mm'am." Homer sat down and the lady tiptoed away, smiling proudly at the important work she had done.

"Members of the Ithaca Parlor Lecture Club," the President of the Club said. "This afternoon we have in store a great treat. Our speaker is to be Rosalie Simms-Pibity." The President of the Club paused, so that there would be time for the customary applause. After the applause, she said, "I do not have to tell you who Rosalie Simms-Pibity is. She is internationally famous—one of the great women of our time. We all know her name and we all know she is famous. But do we, I wonder, know *why* she is famous." The President of the Club answered this question. "I am afraid not. The story of Rosalie Simms-Pibity," she said, as if she were telling a fable not unlike the fable of the Odyssey itself, "is a story *especially* thrilling to women. Simms-Pibity—for that is how she prefers to be known—has lived a life brimming over with adventure, romance, danger, and beauty, and yet today she is scarcely more than a dashing handsome British *girl*—a girl hard as steel and stronger than most men. In fact, there are few men who have lived a life as adventurous as the life of Simms-Pibity."

Now a note of tender sadness came into her voice. "As for us, the stay-at-homes, the mothers, the bringer-uppers, so to speak, of children, the life of Simms-Pibity is like a dream—*our* dream—the unfulfilled dream of each of us who stayed home, gave birth to our children, and looked after our houses. Hers is the beautiful life each of us would have *liked* to have lived if we had dared, but Fate, as it will, has not decreed such adventures for us, and in all the world there is only one Simms-Pibity. Only one!"

The President of the Club paused to look over the faces of her old friends in the audience. "What is it," she said, "that Simms-Pibity has done which has made her so rare among women? Well, the list of her adventures is staggering, and as I read the list, you will scarcely be able to believe any woman could do such things and still be alive, but alive she is, and *here*. Simms-Pibity is going to talk to us in plain language—language perhaps, to some of us, shocking. But first let me go over the adventures—only briefly—for a full recitation of them would take too long, as *every* day is a new adventure for Simms-Pibity. She *creates* adventure wherever she goes, and we may be sure that before she leaves our unknown little city, Ithaca, she will have discovered here things we ourselves do not know.

"From 1915 to 1917 Simms-Pibity drove an ambulance at the front—in the other war. During 1917 and 1918 she went around the world with another girl—on tramp steamers, cattle boats, walking and riding and living in many strange places—sometimes even in native huts. She visited twenty-seven different countries. She was captured by the Southern Army in China as she tried to go overland by river junk and sedan chair from Canton to Hankow." The President of the Club paused a moment to dwell on the magical words, and then repeated them. "Canton and Hankow. Simms-Pibity escaped her capturers by shooting the falls of the Sian River in the wet season when no other boat would go out on the perilous waters.

"In 1919 she went across North Africa from Morocco to Abyssinia. In 1920 she was employed in Syria in the secret service. In Damascus she met King Feisal, who helped her make the exploration of Kufara, never before visited by white people, the secret and sacred capital of the fanatic Senussi Sect, deep in the heart of the Libyan Desert.

Simms-Pibity went disguised as an Egyptian woman one thousand miles on camel-back, her only companions coarse, native men who could speak no English." The President of the Ithaca Parlor Lecture Club lifted her eyes after this remark and looked over at two of her most intimate friends. Homer Macauley wondered what she meant by that glance and then wondered how long she was going to talk about this incredible and wonderful person.

"During 1923," the speaker continued, "Simms-Pibity sailed a twenty-ton dhow with an Arab crew fourteen days down the Red Sea to land at the forbidden port of Jeizan. This time she was disguised as an Arab woman. In 1925 she climbed the Atlas Mountains of Morocco. In 1926 she walked one thousand miles through Abyssinia—perhaps a world record." And then with terrible scorn for herself and her friends, the President of the Ithaca Parlor Lecture Club said, "Do we, I wonder, ever walk with pleasure even so short a distance as the distance from Gottschalk's to Roeding Park?" She sighed and then, not knowing how to answer this question, she offered, "It might perhaps do us good." She returned to the matter of introducing the lecturer of the day, looking for her place in the booklet of notes she held in her hand.

"In 1928 Simms-Pibity covered the Balkans for a London newspaper, disguised now as a native woman of one country, now as a native woman of another."

Getting bored, waiting impatiently, eager to get back to the telegraph office and his work, Homer wondered, "Why is she always disguising herself?"

"In 1930, Simms-Pibity made an exciting journey through Turkey and met Mustapha Kemal, a Turk. There Simms-Pibity was disguised as a young Turkish girl from the hill country. She traveled nine thousand miles on horseback, moving all through the Near East. In Azerbaijan she saw the uprising between the Communist Red Army and the Caucasian peasants. In 1931 she traveled through South America, exploring the jungles of Brazil with only native men for companions, one of whom was named, I understand—from Simms-Pibity herself—Max. But the adventures of Simms-Pibity are endless, and it is *her*

you wish to see and hear, not *me*." This sweet modesty
brought a nervous giggle out of the President of the Club,
followed by sympathetic but hearty laughter from her
friends. When a proper quietude had come over the audience, the President said in a firm and dramatic voice, "It
gives me great pride, as President of the Ithaca Parlor Lecture Club, to present to you—Rosalie Simms-Pibity!"

The applause was swift and loud. The President of the
Club turned toward the wings of the stage to greet the dis-
tinguished visitor, but she wasn't there. The audience, taking advantage of this delay, increased its applause and after perhaps two full minutes of steady hand-clapping—during which a number of women confessed that their hands
were getting sore—the great lady finally presented herself.

Homer expected to see somebody unlike any woman he
had ever before seen. He couldn't imagine what form this
creature would take, but he felt certain that it would be at
least interesting—and so it was. Rosalie Simms-Pibity was
an old woman, horse-faced, dried-out, tall, gaunt, and sex-
less. Because the time had come for Homer to deliver the
telegram, he got to his feet, but perhaps it was because he
was amazed, for he did not run up onto the stage as he had
been instructed to do.

Now, the nice lady who had given him his instructions
came rushing over, and before he knew it she was pushing
him down the aisle and whispering loud enough for everyone to hear, "Now, boy! Deliver the telegram!"

On the stage the great lady pretended not to be aware of
this commotion. "Ladies," she began to say. "Members of
the Ithaca Parlor Lecture Club—" Her voice perfectly suit-
ed her appearance. It was high and shrill.

Homer hurried up onto the stage and in a very clear
voice announced, "Telegram for Rosalie Simms-Pibity!"

The great lady stopped her speech and turned to the
messenger as if his appearance was entirely unplanned.
"Here, boy," she said. "I am Simms-Pibity!" She glanced
back at the audience and said, "Excuse me, ladies." She
signed for the telegram, took it from the messenger, and
then offered him a dime, saying, "And that's for you, boy."

This was painful to Homer, but everything had been so

ridiculous and confusing that he didn't care to bother about refusing it. He took the small coin, dropped it, picked it up, and, very much embarassed, hurried down from the stage, as the woman began her speech.

"Now, in 1939," she said, "just before the outbreak of this new War, I chanced to be in Bavaria on a secret mission, disguised as an Alsatian milkmaid."

In the street, seated on the sidewalk, Homer saw Henry Wilkinson who had lost both legs in a railway accident when he was a young man. Now, thirty years later, he had taken to holding a hat in his lap containing pencils. Homer did not know him by name but he had seen him all his life. Somehow or other, he had never gotten around to buying a pencil or dropping a coin into the hat. Therefore, upon seeing Henry Wilkinson, Homer dropped the dime into the man's hat and hurried to his bicycle.

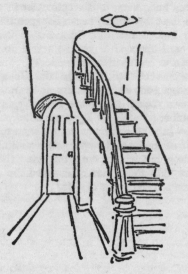

30. At the Bethel Rooms

A HALF HOUR LATER the messenger got off his bicycle at the door of the Bethel Rooms on Eye Street and climbed the long flight of stairs. There was no desk, only a counter in the corner of the spacious hall. On the counter was a solitary press-down bell and a sign on the wall over the bell which said Ring. The messenger looked around, noticing the many closed doors of the small hotel. He then looked at the telegram which was addressed to Dolly Hawthorne. In one of the rooms a phonograph was going, and he could hear two young women and two men talking and laughing.

After a moment a man of forty years or so came out of one of the rooms and stood at the door talking to a young woman whose head alone was visible. Then the door closed quickly and the man went down the stairs. Homer pressed the bell on the counter. The door which had just been closed now opened again and the girl called out, "In a minute." When the girl appeared, the messenger was amazed that she was so beautiful and young. She didn't seem very much different from Mary or Bess.

"Telegram for Dolly Hawthorne," Homer said.

"She's out just now. Can I sign for it?"

"Yes, ma'am." The young woman signed for the telegram and then looked at Homer curiously.

"Wait just a minute, will you?" She ran all the way down the long hall into another room. While she was gone a man came up the stairs and stood at the counter. He and Homer looked at one another several times. When the girl came running back and saw the man, she took Homer by the hand, and they went into the room from which she had first emerged. The room had a strange odor which the messenger had never before known.

The young woman handed the messenger a letter. "Will you mail this letter for me?" She looked the messenger straight in the eye. "It's very important, to my sister. Take it to the Post Office—airmail, special delivery, registered. There's money in the letter. I haven't got any stamps." Now, the young woman stopped a moment so that Homer might have time to understand how important it was for him to properly attend to the mailing of the letter. "Will you do this for me?"

For some reason which he couldn't quite understand, the messenger felt sick. It was the same kind of sickness he had felt in the house of the Mexican woman whose son had been killed in the War.

"Yes, ma'am," Homer said. "I'll take the letter right down to the Post Office—airmail, special delivery, registered."

"Here's a dollar. Put the letter in your hat. Don't let anybody see it. Don't tell *anybody* about it."

"Yes, ma'am. I won't tell anybody." He put the letter in

his hat. "I'll take it straight to the Post Office. Then, I'll bring you the change."

"No, don't come back. Now, hurry! And remember—don't let anybody know."

"I won't," Homer said, and left the room.

He reached the steps just as the girl reached the man at the counter. On the first landing of the stairway Homer came face to face with an enormous, handsomely-dressed woman who was fifty or fifty-five years of age. The woman stopped when she saw the messenger and smiled.

"Telegram for me?" she said. "Dolly Hawthorne?"

"Yes, ma'am," Homer said, "I left it upstairs."

"That's a good boy," Dolly Hawthorne said. She looked at Homer a moment and then said, "You're a new boy, aren't you? Oh, I know all the boys. They're all sweet, nice boys, too—Western Union and Postal both. All the boys are good to me, and I'm good to them." Dolly Hawthorne opened an expensive jeweled handbag and brought out some calling cards. "Here," she said. She handed Homer about twenty of the cards. "You go to a lot of places with telegrams. Bars, and places like that—well, just leave a card on the bar as you go out. Leave them near traveling people—soldiers and sailors who might need a room overnight. With this terrible War going on, we've got to try to make our boys happy as long as they are near us. Nobody knows better than I how lonely a soldier can be, never knowing what's coming next or whether they'll be alive tomorrow or dead."

"Yes, ma'am," Homer said. He went on down the stairs to the street, and Dolly Hawthorne went on up to the Bethel Rooms.

31. Mr. Mechano

AFTER THEIR ADVENTURE at the public library, Lionel
and Ulysses continued to explore Ithaca. At sundown they
found themselves standing in a small crowd of idlers and
passers-by, watching a man in the window of a shabby
drug store. The man moved like a piece of machinery, although he *was* a human being. He looked, however, as if
he had been made of wax instead of flesh. He seemed inhuman and in fact he looked like nothing so much as an
upright, unburied corpse still capable of moving. The man
was the most incredible thing Ulysses had seen in all of his

four years of life in the world. No light came out of
the man's eyes. His lips were set as if they would never
part.

The man was engaged in advertising *Dr. Bradford's
Tonic*. He worked between two easels. On one easel was a
sign on which the following message had been printed:
"Mr. Mechano—The Machine Man—Half Machine, Half
Human. More Dead Than Alive. $50 if you can make him
smile. $500 if you can make him laugh." On the other ea-
sel Mr. Mechano placed pasteboard cards which he took in
an extremely mechanical fashion from the small table in
front of the easel. On these cards were printed various
messages urging people to buy the patent medicine which
Dr. Bradford had invented and thereby to become more
alive. After each new card had been placed on the easel
Mr. Mechano pointed at each word of the message on the
card with a pointer. When all ten of the cards had been
placed on the easel, Mr. Mechano removed them all and
put them back on the table and began the procedure all
over again.

"It's a man," Lionel said. "I can see him. It's not a machine, Ulysses. It's a man! See his eyes? He's alive. See
him?"

The card Mr. Mechano had just placed on the easel
read: "Don't drag yourself around half dead. Enjoy life.
Take Dr. Bradford's Tonic and feel like a new man."

"There's another card," Lionel said. "It says something
on that card." Suddenly he was weary and eager to get
home. "Come on, Ulysses, let's go. We've seen him go
through all the cards three times. Let's go home. It's almost
night now." He took his friend by the hand, but Ulysses
drew his hand away.

"Come on, Ulysses! I've got to go home now. I'm hungry." But Ulysses didn't want to go. It seemed that he
didn't even *hear* Lionel's words.

"I'm going, Ulysses," Lionel challenged. He waited for
Ulysses to turn and go with him, but the boy didn't budge.
A little hurt and amazed by this betrayal of friendship,
Lionel began to walk home, turning every three or four
steps to see if his friend was not going to join him, after

all. But no, Ulysses wanted to stay and watch Mr. Mechano some more. Lionel felt deeply wounded as he continued his journey home. "I thought he was my best friend in the whole world."

Ulysses stood among the handful of people watching Mr. Mechano until at last only he and an old man were left. Mr. Mechano went right on picking up the cards and putting them on the easel. He went right on pointing to each word on each card. Soon the old man went away, too, and then only Ulysses stood on the sidewalk looking up at the strange human being in the window of the drug store. When the street lights came on, Ulysses came out of the trance of fascination into which the vision of Mr. Mechano had placed him. It was almost as if he had become hypnotized by the sight of the man. Now, out of the trance, he looked around. Day had ended and everybody had gone— The only thing left anywhere was something for which he had no word—Death.

The small boy looked back suddenly at the mechanical man. It seemed then and for the first time that the man was looking directly at *him*. There was swift panic and terror in the boy, and then suddenly he was running away. The few people he saw in the streets now seemed full of death, too, like Mr. Mechano. Ulysses ran until he was almost exhausted. He stopped, at last, breathing hard. He looked around, feeling a deep silent steady horror about all things—the horror of Mr. Mechano—Death! He had never before really known fear of *any* kind, let alone fear such as this, and it was the most difficult thing in the world for him to know what to do. His poise was all gone—shattered by the fear of the horror catching up with *him*, and he began to run again. This time as he ran he said to himself, almost crying, "Papa, Mama, Marcus, Bess, Homer!"

The world had been wonderful and full of good things to see again and again, but now the world was a thing to escape, only he could think of no direction to take. He wanted swiftly to reach somebody of his family. He stood panic-stricken, and then began moving a few steps in one direction and then a few in another, feeling all around him a presence of incredible disaster, a disaster he could escape only by reaching his father, his mother, one of his brothers, or his sister. And then, instead of reaching one of these, he saw far down the street the leader of the neighborhood gang, August Gottlieb. The newsboy was standing on a deserted street corner, calling out the headline as if the area around him were full of people who must be told what had happened that day in the world. Hollering headlines had always seemed slightly ridiculous to August Gottlieb because, for one thing, the headlines were always about murder of one sort or another and, for another, it seemed somehow a thing of bad manners to go about among people in the streets of Ithaca lifting his voice. Consequently, the newsboy felt pleased when at last he discovered that the streets were deserted. Without even knowing that he was doing such a thing, whenever the streets had become empty of the people of Ithaca, August Gottlieb, as if grateful for his almost solitary inhabitance of the city, lifted his voice more powerfully than ever, calling out the day's miserable news. What could a man do about the news—sell a paper, and make a few pennies? Is that what he could do? Wasn't it foolish for him to cry out the daily message of mistake as if it were glad tidings? Wasn't it shameful for the people to be so steadily unimpressed by every day's new crimes? Sometimes even in his sleep the newsboy dreamed of calling out the headlines of the world's news, but there, in that inner area of experience, he felt contempt for the nature of the news, and when he shouted, it was always from a great height, and beneath him always were multitudes engaged in frantic activities of error and wrong-doing. But the minute they heard his voice, they stopped in their tracks to look up at him, and then he always shouted, "Now go back, go back where you belong! Stop your killing! Plant trees instead!" He had always loved the idea of trees.

When Ulysses saw August Gottlieb on the corner, some of the terror in his heart passed away. He wanted to call out to Auggie, but he couldn't make a sound. Instead, he ran with all his might to the newsboy and flung himself upon him in an embrace so forceful that it almost knocked Auggie down.

"Ulysses!" the newsboy said. "What's the matter? What are you crying about?"

Ulysses looked up into the eyes of the newsboy, but still he couldn't speak.

"You're scared about something. Well, don't be. There's nothing to be scared of. Now, stop crying." Auggie waited, and Ulysses tried very hard to stop. Soon the sobs came at infrequent intervals, each sob like a hiccup. Then Auggie said, "Come on, Ulysses, I'll take you to Homer."

At the sound of that name, the name of his brother, Ulysses smiled at last, and then hiccuped another sob. "Homer?"

"Sure. Come on."

It was almost too wonderful for the little boy to believe. "Going to see Homer?"

"Sure. The telegraph office is just around the corner."

August Gottlieb and Ulysses Macauley walked into the telegraph office. They found Homer seated at the delivery desk. When Ulysses saw his brother, a wonderful thing happened to his face. All the terror left his eyes, because now he was home.

When Homer saw his brother, he turned to Auggie. "What's Ulysses doing in town at this hour?"

"He got lost, I guess. He was crying."

"Crying?" Homer said, and then lifted and hugged his brother, just as Ulysses hiccuped another sob. "All right, I'll take you home on my bike."

From his desk the manager of the telegraph office, Thomas Spangler, watched the three boys, and the old telegraph operator, William Grogan, stopped his work to watch them, too. They looked at one another several times. Homer put his brother down. He knew the boy was all right again when Ulysses went to the delivery desk to look at things there. Homer put his arm around August and said, "Thanks, Auggie."

Spangler got up and went to the boys. "Let me have a paper, Auggie."

"Yes, sir," Auggie said, and began to go through the routine of folding the paper and making the sale, but Spangler stopped him, so that he could hold the paper out be-

fore him. The manager of the telegraph office glanced at
the headline, and then threw the paper into the wastebasket. "How's it going?"

"I've made fifty-five cents so far, but I started at one
o'clock. When I make seventy-five cents I'm going home."

"Why?" Spangler said. "Why do you want to make seventy-five cents?"

"I don't know," Auggie said. "I just thought I ought to
make seventy-five cents on a Saturday. There's nobody in
town hardly, but I think I can sell the rest of my papers in
another hour or two. Pretty soon people start coming back
to town after supper—the movie crowd."

"Well, the hell with the movie crowd. Give me the rest
of your papers and go home *now*. Here's a quarter."

Even though the newsboy felt grateful to the manager
for this gesture, somehow it didn't seem right to him.
What it came to was that you really had to sell papers one
at a time and each one to a different person, and you had
to stand on a street corner and holler the headline and
make the people *want* to buy a paper and read the news.
He was tired, and he wanted to get home to supper, and he
never did know anybody like Spangler before, but it just
didn't seem right, somehow.

"I don't want to make a quarter from *you*, Mr. Spangler."

"Never mind," Spangler insisted. "Give me the papers
and go home."

"Yes, sir," Auggie said. "But maybe you'll let me do
something for you some day."

"Sure," Spangler said, and threw the papers into the
wastebasket.

Auggie turned to go home, but Homer stopped him.
"Wait a minute, I'll hike you home. Is it all right, Mr.
Spangler? I've got a pickup at Ithaca Wine, and it's on the
way home. So if it's all right, I'll hike Ulysses and Auggie
home and then go and get the pickup at Ithaca Wine. Is it
all right?"

"Sure," Spangler said, and went back to his desk.

"You don't need to hike me home," Auggie said. "Hiking

two people at one time is too much. I can walk it in no time."

"You can't walk it in no time. It's almost two miles. I can hike both of you very easily. You can sit on the frame and Ulysses can sit on the handlebars. Now, come on."

The three boys went out to Homer's bicycle. The load was a heavy one, especially for a man with one bad leg, but Homer got his passengers safely home. They stopped first at the little house next door to Ara'a Market—Auggie's house. Ara himself was standing in front of the store, holding the hand of his little boy. They were looking up into the sky. Down the street, next to the empty lot, Mrs. Macauley stood in the yard under the old walnut tree, taking clothes off the line. Mary and Bess were in the parlor playing and singing, and the sound of the piano and Mary's voice could be heard faintly.

Auggie got off the bicycle and went into his house. Homer stood a moment in the street, holding the bike and looking up at the sky and over at the Macauley house. Then, Auggie came out of the house and went up to Ara, the grocer.

"Did you do a lot of business today, Mr. Ara?"

"Thank you, Auggie, I am satisfied."

"I've got seventy-five cents I want to spend. I want to get a lot of things for tomorrow."

"All right, Auggie," the grocer said, but before turning and going back into the store he pointed to the clouds in the sky and then looked at his son. "See, John? Nighttime come now—pretty soon we get in our beds, go to sleep. Sleep all night. When daytime come, we get up again. New day."

The grocer and his son and the neighbor boy went into the store. In the meantime, Ulysses, sitting on the handlebars of his brother's bicycle, was watching his mother. Now, Homer got back onto the bicycle and began to ride toward the house.

As they drew closer to the woman in the yard under the tree, the little brother's face filled with light, but at the same time there was now a deep sadness in the face.

Homer rode straight across the empty lot into the backyard, under the walnut tree. He got off the bicycle and set Ulysses down on his feet. Ulysses stood looking at his mother. Gone from him now almost as if forever was the terror that had come from Mr. Mechano.

"He got lost," Homer said. "Auggie found him and brought him to the telegraph office. I can't stay, but I'll go in and say hello to Bess and Mary."

Homer went into the house and stood in the dark dining room, listening to his sister and the girl his brother loved. When the song was over, he moved into the parlor.

The two girls turned. "I got a letter from Marcus to-day," Mary said.

"How is he?"

"Just fine. They're going away soon, but they don't know where. He says not to worry if we don't get any more letters for a while."

"He wrote to all of us," Bess said, "to Mama, and me, and even to Ulysses."

Homer waited a moment for the announcement of the arrival of *his* letter, afraid there might not be such an announcement. At last he said very quietly, "Didn't he send *me* a letter, too?"

"Oh, of course," Bess said. "Yours is the heaviest letter of all. I thought you'd *know* that if he wrote to all of us, he'd write to you, too."

Homer's sister lifted a letter off the table and handed it to him. Homer looked at the letter a long time and then his sister said, "Well, why don't you open it and read it? Read it to us."

"No, Bess, I've got to go now. I'll take it to the office and read it there tonight when I've got a lot of time."

"We spent the whole day looking for a job," Bess said, "but we didn't find one."

"We had a lot of fun just the same," Mary said. "It was a lot of fun just going in and asking."

"Well, fun or no fun," Homer said, "I'm glad you didn't find a job. I make all the money this family needs, and Mary's father's got a good job at Ithaca Wine. You two don't need to go looking for a job."

"Yes, we do," Bess said. "And one of these days we're

going to find one. Two places asked us to come back."

"Never mind finding a job," Homer said. He was angry now. "Any work that has to be done around here, men can do. Girls belong in homes, taking care of men, that's all." He was thinking of the beautiful girl at the Bethel Rooms. "Just because there happens to be a war in the world isn't any reason for everybody to go out of their heads. Just stay home where you belong and help Mama, and you help your father, Mary."

He was so bossy, his sister Bess was almost proud of him, because never before had she seen him so concerned about *anything*.

He went back to the dark dining room.

Bess began to play the piano, and soon Mary began to sing. The messenger stood in the dark room listening, but before the song was half finished he went quietly out of the house. Now, in the yard, he found Ulysses standing over the hen nest looking down at one egg.

"Egg," Ulysses said as if the word were also the word for God, Himself.

Homer got onto his bicycle and began riding to Ithaca Wine.

32. On the Train

As HOMER RODE his bicycle, far away an American passenger train moved swiftly through the night. The train was filled with American boys in uniform.

Some of the boys were past forty, even, but most of them were kids—from big cities and little towns, from farms and offices, from rich families and poor families, some taken away from great dreams of achievement and some from humble dreams of peace—kids brilliant and swift in spirit and kids slow and steady. In the midst of the clamor, laughter, excitement, fear, doubt, confusion, eagerness, and the magnificent combination of profound ignorance and profound wisdom, Marcus Macauley and his friend Tobey George talked quietly.

"Well," Tobey said, "I guess we're on our way, at last."

"Most likely," Marcus said.

"I don't know about you, Marcus, but I feel lucky, because if it hadn't been for this War and the Draft I wouldn't have run into you, and I would never have found out about your family."

Marcus felt embarassed. "I feel the same way about you." He stopped a moment and then asked the question that every man exposed to unknown danger must ask himself again and again. "I want you to tell me the truth. Are you afraid of being killed?"

The other could not answer the question immediately, but at last he said, "Sure, I am. I could bluff, I guess, and *pretend* that I'm not. But I am. Aren't you?"

"Very afraid," Marcus said. "But if you're lucky, what do you want to get back to?"

"I don't know," Toby said, because he didn't know. "I guess I want to get back to whatever it happens to be. I haven't got a family, as you have. I haven't anybody to go back to, but whatever it is, that'll be O.K. with me. I haven't got a girl waiting for me like you've got Mary, but I know I want to get back just the same—if I can."

"Right," Marcus said. "How does it happen that you like to sing?"

"How should I know? I just like to sing, that's all." They listened to the train and to the noise inside the train, and then Tobey said, "What do *you* think about?"

Marcus took a little time before trying to answer this question. "Ithaca," he said at last.

"It's a funny thing," Tobey said. "Maybe you won't understand a thing like this, but I feel that Ithaca is *my* home town, too. If we come out of this O.K., will you take me to Ithaca?"

"Sure," Marcus said. "And I want you to meet my family. My father was some kind of a great man, I think. I don't mean successful or important or anything like that. He didn't even have a trade or a profession. He just worked for a living. Any kind of a job. He never made any more money than we needed, but I think he was great, just the same."

"Matthew Macauley?" Tobey said.

"He worked in the vineyards, in the packing houses, and in the wineries. Plain, ordinary, everyday work. If you saw him in the street you'd think he was nobody, but he was my father, and I know different. The only thing he cared about was his family—my mother, and his kids. He saved money for months and made a down payment on a harp—think of it, a harp. Nobody plays a harp any more, but that's what my mother wanted. It took him five years to pay for it. It was the most expensive harp you could buy. We used to think every house had a harp just because we had one. Then, he bought a piano for my sister Bess—that didn't cost so much. I thought everybody was like my father—until I got out and met some of the others."

"I wish I knew somebody like that," Tobey said. "He wouldn't have to be *my* father, he could be anybody, just so I *knew* him."

"Maybe your father *was* great."

"Maybe. Want to hear something funny? I didn't know kids had mothers and fathers until I went to school and heard the other kids talk about them. I thought every man was in the world alone—the same as me—to start out all by himself. I guess I felt bad for a long time, after I found out. Maybe *that's* the reason I like to sing. You don't feel so—out of everything—so alone when you're singing." Then shyly, almost timidly, he said, "What kind of a girl is Bess?"

Marcus knew his friend felt uncomfortable about asking the question. "You can ask me about my sister. I'd like you to meet her someday. I think she'll like you."

"Me?" Tobey said.

"Yes, I think she'll like you very much. I'd like you to stay at our house. If you like each other—well, I just think she'll like you very much, that's all."

Now, Marcus began to speak swiftly, because while he knew it was almost impossible to speak of such a thing at all, he also knew it was necessary to *try* to do so, at least.

"If it happens that you like her, too—well, what I mean is, marry her and live in Ithaca. It's a good town. You can make a good life there. Now, here. I'm going to give you her picture—to keep." He handed Tobey a little snapshot of his sister. "Keep it in your identification folder where I keep Mary's picture. See?"

Tobey George looked at the snapshot for a long time, while Marcus looked at him. At last he said, "Bess sure is beautiful. I don't know if a guy can fall in love with a girl without meeting her, even, but I feel in love with Bess already. I feel sick. I'll tell you the truth. I was afraid to talk to you about Bess until now. But I figured, well, maybe as long as we're on our way, and there's no telling, you might not mind so much. I can't help it, but I always feel I haven't got the same kind of rights that other people have—you know, a guy who was given his name by an orphanage, not by his mother and father—who doesn't even know who his mother and father are—who doesn't even know what nationality they are—or what nationality *he* is. Some people say I'm Spanish and French, and some people say I'm Italian and Greek, and some people say I'm English and Irish. Almost everybody gives me a different nationality."

"You're an American," Marcus said. "That's all. Any man can see that. Now keep that picture. We'll go back to Ithaca and you'll raise a family and I'll raise a family, and we'll visit each other once in a while, have some music and songs—pass the time of life."

"You know, Marcus," Tobey said, "I *believe* you. I swear to God I believe you. I don't think you're saying this just because we happen to be friends, on our way. I believe you, and more than anything else in the world I want to go to Ithaca. I want to live there and I want to do all the things you said." He stopped a moment to try to imagine what might go wrong to keep him from doing these things, and then he said, "If Bess doesn't like me—if she falls in love with somebody else—if she's married when we get there—I'm going to live in Ithaca, anyway. I don't know, but Ithaca seems to be *my* home now, too. For the first time in my life I feel that I belong somewhere and—I hope you won't mind—I feel that my family is the Macau-

ley family, because that's the kind of family I'd want for
myself if I could choose. I hope to God Bess does like me,
or doesn't fall in love with someone else, because I *know* I
like *her*." Now, he spoke very softly, and even though the
train was full of noise, Marcus could hear the words,
"Ithaca's my home. That's where I live. That's where I
want to be when I die—if I can."

Now, the friends were greeted by other boys, and they
shouted with the others, and even sang a song which several of the boys themselves had invented, a song about wom-
en of the streets and what they were good for. And then in
the midst of this singing, Tobey said, "At the orphanage,
we were *forced* to pray. It was a rule there. Whether we
wanted to or not, we prayed."

"That's not such a bad rule," Marcus said, "but of
course prayer is one thing you can't really force."

"I guess that's why I quit praying when I left the orphanage. I don't think I've said a prayer since I was thirteen years old. But I'm starting all over again, as of right
now—and this is it." Tobey waited a moment and then, without closing his eyes, without bowing his head, without
folding his hands, he began to pray, and what he said was
unmistakably a prayer. "Just get me to Ithaca, if You can.
Anything You say, but if You can, get me to Ithaca. Let
me get home. Protect everybody. Keep everybody out of
pain. Find homes for the homeless. Get the traveler safely
home and get me to Ithaca. Amen!"

"That's a good prayer," Marcus said. "I hope it's answered."

Now, the soldiers were singing another song. This one
had to do with the impermanence of all things, particularly
a woman's love, and the boys delighted in the cynical
wisdom of the song. Tobey and Marcus joined in the singing, and then suddenly Tobey said, "What do *you* pray
for?"

"The same things you pray for—the very same things."

After the song everybody became silent. There was no
reason for this silence and yet every man on the train was
suddenly unaccountably hushed. At last a soldier named
Joe Higgins came to Marcus and Tobey and said, "What

the hell's the matter, what's everybody so quiet about? How about a *real* song, Tobey? How about playing for us on the accordion, Marcus?"

"What would you like to hear?" Marcus said.

"Oh, I don't know. We've sung all the dirty songs, maybe we ought to sing something old—you know, something *good!* Why don't we sing a good old-time church song—something we all know from when we were kids?"

"What church song do you know, Joe?"

"Well," Joe said. "Now don't you guys laugh. I know *Leaning.* You know—*Leaning on the Everlasting Arms.*"

"Do you know the words of that song, Tobey? If you don't, I can help you."

"Do I *know* them?" Tobey said. "I guess I sang that song almost every Sunday for ten years."

"All right," Marcus said, "let's do it for Joe. If you feel like joining in, Joe, you don't have to know how to sing. Just join in, that's all."

"Oh, I'm going to sing *that* song all right."

Marcus began to play the old hymn, and soon Tobey began to sing:

"What a fellowship, what a joy divine,
  Leaning on the everlasting arms;
  What a blessedness, what a peace is mine,
  Leaning on the everlasting arms."

Now, in a strong, unmusical but nevertheless pleasant voice, Joe began to sing with Tobey, and soon everybody in the train was listening. After a moment everybody gathered around Marcus and Tobey and Joe to be nearer the music, as Joe and Tobey sang:

"Leaning, leaning, safe and secure from all alarms;
  Leaning, leaning, leaning on the everlasting arms."

By this time everybody was singing.

33. Marcus

THIS SATURDAY was one of the longest and most eventful days of Homer Macauley's life. Little things began to take on fresh importance and to mean something he could understand. The sleep of last night, troubled and full of sorrow, was now forever a part of his wakefulness. He had tried with all his might to keep the messenger of Death from reaching Ithaca and its people. He had dreamed that, but now it was no longer a dream.

The letter from his brother Marcus was in the pocket of his blue messenger's jacket waiting to be opened and read.

He came into the telegraph office, limping, tired and eager to rest. He looked at the call sheet, and there were no calls to take. He looked on the incoming telegram hook and there were no telegrams to deliver. All was clear. He went to the old telegraph operator and said, "Mr. Grogan, would you like to chip in for two day-old pies—apple and cocoanut cream?"

"I'll chip in, my boy, but I'll not have any of the pies—thanks just the same."

"If *you* don't want any of the pies, Mr. Grogan, I don't want any, either. I thought *you* might be hungry. I'm not hungry at all. I haven't had a chance to take it easy all day, but I'm not hungry. It seems funny. You'd think a fellow would get hungry working all day and all night, but sometimes he doesn't."

"How's your leg?"

"O.K., I've forgotten all about it. I get around all right." He looked curiously at the old man and then said very softly, "Are you drunk, Mr. Grogan?" He spoke earnestly, and the old man wasn't offended or hurt.

"Yes, I am, my boy." Mr. Grogan went to his chair and sat down. After a moment he looked over at the boy across the table from him, not sitting but standing there. "I feel a lot better when I'm drunk." Then, he brought the bottle out and took a good long drink. "I'm not going to tell you never to take a drink. I'm not going to say, as so many old fools do—*Learn a lesson from me. Look what drink did to me.* You're getting around now, seeing a lot of things you never saw before. Well, let me tell you something. Anything that concerns people—be very careful about. If you see something you're sure is wrong, *don't* be sure. If it's people, be very careful. Now, you'll forgive me, but I must tell you, because you're a man I respect, so I don't mind trying to tell you that it's not right to criticize the way *any* people happen to be. As a man gets closer to the end of his time he feels glad about the people he knows who're going to go on when he's gone. Can you understand what I'm saying?"

"I'm not sure, Mr. Grogan."

"I'm telling you something I couldn't tell you unless I *were* drunk.

"I'm telling you this—be grateful for yourself. Yes, for *yourself*. Be thankful. Understand that what a man is is something he *can* be grateful for, and *ought* to be grateful for. Be thankful that the man you are will be trusted by total strangers."

Again Homer remembered the girl at Bethel Rooms, and the urgent way she spoke to him, as if to an old friend.

"They will know you will not betray them or hurt them. They will know that you will not despise them. That you will see in them what everybody else has failed to see. You must know that about yourself. You must not be embarassed by it. You are a man, fourteen years old. Who has made you such a man, I don't know, but as it's true, know that it's true, and be grateful for yourself. Do you understand?"

The messenger gulped. "I guess so, Mr. Grogan."

"Then, I thank you. What's that you're holding—a letter? I have finished. Go ahead. Read your letter, boy."

"From my brother Marcus. I haven't had a chance to open it yet."

"Then, open it. Read the letter from your brother. Read it aloud."

"Aloud?"

"Yes, I'd like to hear it, if I may. Very much."

Homer tore open the envelope, brought out the letter, unfolded it, and began to read, speaking very slowly.

"Dear Homer: First of all, everything of mine at home is yours—to give to Ulysses when you no longer want them: my books, my phonograph, my records, my clothes when you're ready to fit into them, my bicycle, my microscope, my fishing tackle, my collection of rocks from Piedra, and all the other things of mine at home. They're yours because you are now the man of the Macauley family of Ithaca. The money I made last year at the packing house I have given to Ma of course, to help out. It is not nearly enough, though. I don't know how you are going to be able to keep our family together and go to high school at the same time, but I believe you will find a way. My

Army pay goes to Ma, except for a few dollars that I must have, but this money is not enough, either. It isn't easy for me to hope for so much from you, when I myself did not begin to work until I was nineteen, but somehow I believe that you will be able to do what I didn't do.

"I miss you of course and I think of you all the time. I am O.K., and even though I have never believed in wars —and know them to be foolish, even when they are necessary—I am proud that I am involved, since so many others are, and this is what's happening. I do not recognize any enemy which is human, for no human being can be my enemy. Whoever he is, he is my friend. My quarrel is not with *him*, but with that unfortunate part of him which I seek to destroy in myself first.

"I do not feel like a hero. I have no talent for such feelings. I hate no one. I do not feel patriotic either, for I have always loved my country, its people, its towns, my home, and my family. I would rather I were not in the Army. I would rather there were no War. I have no idea what is ahead, but whatever it is I am resigned and ready for it. I am terribly afraid—I must tell *you* this—but I believe that when the time comes I shall do what is right for me. I shall obey no command other than the command of my own heart. With me will be boys from all over America, from thousands of towns like Ithaca. I may be killed, of course. We all know that. I don't like the idea at all. More than anything else in the world I want to come back to Ithaca. I want to come back for Mary and a home and a family of my own. We leave soon—for action, but nobody knows where the action will be. Therefore, this may be my last letter to you for some time. I hope it's not the last of all, but if it is, hold us together. I have told my friend Tobey George about Ithaca and our family. Some day I hope to bring him to Ithaca. I am glad that I am the Macauley who is involved in this War, for it would be a pity and a mistake if it were you.

"I can say in a letter what I could never say in speech. You are the best of the Macauleys. Nothing must stop you. Now I will write your name here, to remind you: Homer Macauley. That's who you are. I miss you. I can't wait to see you again. God bless you. So long. Your brother, Marcus."

While he was reading the letter the messenger sat down. He read very slowly, gulping and becoming sick many times, as he had become sick in the house of the Mexican mother. Now, he got up. His hands were trembling. He bit the corner of his lower lip and looked over at the old telegraph operator. He spoke very softly. "If my brother is killed in this stupid War, I shall spit at the world. I shall hate it forever."

Tears came to his eyes. He hurried to the locker behind the repeater rack, took off his uniform and got into his regular clothes. He was running out of the office almost before his clothes had been properly arranged.

The old telegraph operator sat a long time. It was very quiet when he shook himself at last, finished the rest of the bottle, got up and looked around the office.

34. At the Church

THE PATTERN OF LIFE in Ithaca—of people everywhere in the world, for that matter—followed a design which at first seemed senseless and perhaps even crazy, but as the days and nights gathered together as months and years, the pattern was seen to have had some semblance of form and meaning.

Many times the telegraph box rattled and Mr. Grogan sat at the typewriter and tapped out a message of love or hope, or pain, or death from the world to its children. "I am coming home." "Happy birthday." "The Department of War regrets to inform you that your son is dead." "Meet me at the Southern Pacific Depot." "Here is a kiss." "I am all right." "God bless you." Many times Homer Macauley delivered the messages.

In the parlor of the Macauley house the strings of the harp were plucked and the message of song was heard. The soldiers moved on, over land, over water, through the air, under the water, into new places, new days, new nights, new sleep, and new and strange moments filled with incredible noises and dangers. The faces of the living changed, but imperceptibly—Marcus, Tobey, Homer, Spangler, Grogan, Mrs. Macauley, Ulysses, Diana, Auggie, Lionel, Bess, Mary, the girl at the Bethel Rooms, Rosalie Simms-Peabody, Mr. Ara, his son John, Big Chris, Miss Hicks, and even Mr. Mechano.

The freight train with the Negro leaning over the side of the gondola moved on. The gopher peeked out of the earth. The apricots of Mr. Henderson's tree took on the smiling color of the sun and the freckles of the boys who came to steal them. The brooding hen came forth with her nation of chicks. Ulysses watched. The limp in Homer's leg healed. Easter Sunday came to Ithaca. And then the Sunday after Easter. And then another Sunday, and then another, and another, and another.

All of the Macauleys of Ithaca sat with Mary Arena on *this* Sunday in the First Ithaca Presbyterian Church. Ulysses sat on the aisle. Directly in front of him, by religious accident, sat a man with a bald head. This living ball which was the better part of a man was fascinating for Ulysses to behold: the shape alone was something to study, being not unlike the shape of the egg. The half dozen hairs of the head, growing in a lonely group, were unashamed and heroic. The wrinkle which divided the head as the equator divides the earth was a miracle of design.

Now, Reverend Holly and the congregation were engaged in a pious oral duel—on the theme of the Blessed Life. First, Reverend Holly read a verse, then, the congregation answered in one voice.

"And seeing the multitudes," Reverend Holly said, "He

went up into a mountain, and when He was seated, His disciples came unto Him.

"*And He opened His mouth,*" the congregation replied: "*and taught them, saying:*

"Blessed are the poor: for theirs is the kingdom of heaven.

"*Blessed are they that mourn: for they shall be comforted.*

"Blessed are the meek: for they shall inherit the earth.

"*Blessed are they which do hunger and thirst after righteousness: for they shall be filled.*

"Blessed are the merciful: for they shall obtain mercy.

"*Blessed are the pure in heart: for they shall see God.*

"Blessed are the peacemakers: for they shall be called the children of God.

"*Rejoice, and be exceeding glad: Ye are the salt of the earth. Ye are the light of the world.*

"Let your light so shine before men that they may see your good works and glorify your Father which is in heaven."

The responsive reading had begun while Ulysses was studying the bald head. Suddenly this object was decorated by a fly which began to explore the head, apparently looking for something recently lost. Ulysses watched the fly, and then reached out to catch it, but Mrs. Macauley took his hand and held it. Staring steadily at the bald head and the fly, thinking of nothing in particular, and then falling away into a daydream, Ulysses now saw the smooth skin of the head as a desert. He saw the wrinkle across the head as a stream, the group of seven hairs as palm trees, and the fly as a lion. Then he saw himself, in his Sunday clothes, on one side of the stream, with the lion on the other. He stood on the bank of the stream looking across at the lion, which in turn came directly opposite to look at *him.* The Scripture reading continued.

In the distance Ulysses saw an Arab, in flowing robes, lying asleep upon the sand. Beside the Arab was a mandolin, or some such musical instrument, and a pitcher of water. Ulysses saw the lion, in a peace and innocence not unlike the sleeping man's, move to the man's head and bend down to smell the man, but not to harm him. As a matter of fact, he had seen the picture in one of the books Lionel had opened at the public library.

The Scripture reading ended. The church organ breathed deeply, and the choir and the congregation began to sing a song in which Ulysses heard the words, And he walks with me and he talks with me. The lion in the desert, of course. And then *Rock of Ages*.

The vision of the lion walking and talking in the desert vanished from the little boy's dream. In its place appeared an ocean. Clinging to a rock which rose several feet above the surface of this desolation of water was Ulysses himself. Only his head and hands were above water. He looked around for escape or rescue, but all that he could see was water. Even so, he was patient and full of faith. At last, far in the distance, walking on the water, Ulysses saw the great man, Big Chris. Big Chris came to Ulysses and without a word reached down to him, took him by the hand and lifted him out of the water onto the surface of it. After a moment, however, Ulysses fell back into the water, splashing, and once again Big Chris fished him out and set him on his feet. Holding the boy's hand, Big Chris went walking upon the water with Ulysses. Far away, the towers of a great white city became visible and around the city, earth and vegetation. The man and the boy walked toward the city.

The song ended. Suddenly somebody was shaking Ulysses. He woke with a start. It was Lionel—with a collection plate. Ulysses found his nickel, placed it in the plate, and passed the plate to his mother.

Lionel whispered to Ulysses, speaking with an air of piety and mystery. "Are you saved, Ulysses?"

"What?"

"Read this," Lionel said, and handed his friend a religious pamphlet.

Ulysses studied the pamphlet, but of course couldn't read the big letters which formed the following words: "Are you saved? It is never too late."

On the other side of the aisle Lionel asked an elderly gentleman the same question. "Are you saved?"

The man looked at the boy severely and then whispered, "Go along, boy."

Before going, however, and somewhat in the manner of a missionary despised by an African tribal chief, Lionel offered the elderly gentleman one of the pamphlets. The elderly gentleman, irritated, grabbed the pamphlet out of Lionel's hands.

The elderly gentleman's wife whispered, "What is it, dear?"

"The boy asked me if I was saved. Then, he offered me *this*." The man handed the pamphlet to his wife who patted his hand and said, "How should the boy know you've been a missionary in China for thirty years?"

All during the ritual of taking collection, the organ played softly and a soprano sang. Lionel, Auggie, Shag and a number of the other boys of Ithaca stood at the back of the center aisle, each holding a collection plate, until the music ended. Then, in ritualistic silence and earnestness the boys marched down the aisle to the table directly beneath the pulpit, where they put the collection plates one on top of the other, and then returned to their places beside their parents.

35. The Lion in the Net

AFTER CHURCH and Sunday dinner, August Gottlieb was in his front yard patching an old tennis net into something he hoped might turn out to be useful. Enoch Hopper, a boy of Auggie's age, came by swiftly, stopped swiftly, and watched swiftly. He was the owner of an old baseball with the cover gone, which he slammed onto the sidewalk fiercely, making it bounce very high. He caught the ball and slammed it again. Enoch Hopper was the most high-strung boy in Ithaca, the most restless, the swiftest-moving, the most impatient, and the loudest-talking.

"What are you making, Auggie?"

"Net."

"What for? Fish?"

"No, animals."

Already Enoch was bored. "Come on, let's start a baseball game or go out to Guggenheim's water tank and climb it."

"Got to fix the net."

"Ah, what've you got to fix the net for?"

"Catch animals."

"Where do you see any animals around here? Come on, let's go. Let's go out to Malaga and go swimming."

"I'll catch animals in this net all right."

"Couldn't catch *a flea* with that tennis net. Come on, let's start a game. Let's go down and sneak into the Bijou, see a Tarzan picture."

"I'll catch a dog first, just to see how it works. And then, watch out!"

"Ah, that's an old tennis net, Auggie. You won't catch anything. Let's go down to the courthouse park, to the city jail there and talk to the prisoners."

"I've got to fix my animal net," Auggie said. "I'm only going to try it out today—and then oh, boy—tomorrow!"

"Oh, boy, *what?*" Enoch said. "There's no animals around here. A cow. A couple of dogs. Six or seven rabbits. A few chickens—what are you going to catch?"

"I got a good net here. Big enough for a bear."

"You couldn't catch a teddy-bear with that net. Let's go down to Chinatown and walk down China Alley."

August Gottlieb interrupted his work a moment to think about Chinatown and the Chinese. He looked up at Enoch Hopper and said, "You afraid of the Chinese?"

"Naaah," Enoch said truthfully. "I ain't afraid of nobody. Even if they were dangerous they couldn't catch *me*. Too fast on my feet."

"I bet a lion could catch you."

"Naaah. I'm too fast. A lion couldn't get anywhere near me. Bears, tigers, Chinese—I'm too fast for 'em. Come on, let's go over across the Southern Pacific tracks and get into a game with the Cosmos Playground gang."

"A trap could catch you."

"No trap in the world fast enough to catch me. Let's go out to the fair grounds and run around the mile track. I'll give you a hundred yards headstart."

"Your own father could catch you."

"Naaah, couldn't come anywhere near me. I'd leave him in the dust."

Now, Lionel came along from his house. "What are you making, Auggie?"

"Net, to catch animals."

"Couldn't catch a flea with that net," Enoch said. "Come on, let's go out on the empty lot and play catch."

"Me?" Lionel said.

"Sure, Lionel. Come on. You throw 'em to me real hard. I'll throw 'em to you real easy. Come on, half the afternoon's gone."

"All right, Enoch," Lionel said, "but remember—throw 'em easy. I ain't so good at catch. Sometimes I miss and the ball hits me in the face. Hurt my eyes once, my nose twice."

"I'll throw 'em easy. Don't worry. Come on."

Enoch Hopper and Lionel Cabot moved across the street to the empty lot, and Auggie went ahead with his work. Soon he had all of the pieces of the old tennis net tied together, so that there was an almost square piece of netting. He stretched this netting out and attached each corner to a stick in the ground so that he could behold what he had made. Now, Shag Manoogian came over the backyard fence. "What's that?"

"Net, to catch animals. Want to help me try it out?"

"Sure. How does it work?"

"Well," Auggie said, "I'll hold the net and hide here behind Ara's store. You call Enoch. He's over there playing catch with Lionel. Enoch is swifter and harder to catch than a lion. If this net can hold Enoch, it can hold anything. All right. I'm hiding. Call Enoch. Tell him you want to ask him something. I'm ready."

"O.K.," Shag said. He looked over at Enoch on the empty lot and then called out, "Enoch! Oh, Enoch!"

Enoch Hopper turned and shouted back, twice as loud, "What do you want, Shag?"

"Come here. I want to ask you something."

"What do you want to ask me?"

"I'll tell you when you get here."

"O.K." Enoch began to run toward Shag, while Lionel followed, not quite sure whether he should run or walk.

"All right, Shag," Auggie whispered. "Duck back here and hide with me. Take hold of this end of the net. When he comes around the corner of the store we'll jump on him and capture him. See?"

Running swiftly, Enoch shouted, "Let's go out to Malaga and swim. Half the afternoon's gone already. Let's do something. What are we waiting for?"

He came running around the corner of Mr. Ara's market. Auggie and Shag leaped out swiftly and spread the net over him. Sure enough, Enoch Hopper moved like an undomesticated animal, perhaps a lion. The two big-game hunters worked furiously but the net wasn't quite strong enough, and soon Enoch Hopper was standing upright, completely unoffended by the unsuccessful experiment.

He slammed the baseball on the sidewalk. "Come on, Auggie, let's go! That net couldn't catch a flea! Come on! What are we waiting for?"

"O.K.," Auggie said, and threw the net into the yard. "Let's go to the courthouse park and talk to the prisoners."

Auggie, Enoch, Shag, and Lionel moved on down the street toward the courthouse park. Soon Enoch Hopper was a block ahead of the others, shouting back at them, "Come on! What are you guys moving so slow for?" He slammed the baseball on the sidewalk.

36. Spangler

THOMAS SPANGLER and Diana Steed were in the country for a Sunday afternoon drive around Kingsburg. The car was an old red roadster with the top down.

"Those," he said, pointing to a row of trees bordering a vineyard, "are fig trees. The vines beyond them are Muscat vines. There's some olive trees. That tree's a pomegranate. Those vines over there are Malaga vines. There's an orchard of peach trees. These are apricots. There's a walnut tree. There's a tree you don't see very often—persimmon. *Everything* grows in this valley."

"Oh, darling," Diana said, "you do love trees, don't you?"

"Yes, I do, and we're going to have ourselves at least two of each on our own little place, so the kids can climb them and take fruit off of them, and eat the fruit."

"Oh, darling, you are happy, aren't you?"

"Never been happier."

He put his arm around her. "I can't wait to see who it is. I'd like it to be a little girl. I'd like to hear the voice of a little girl like that. I used to think you were scatter-brained. Well, anybody who can do *that* can't be scatter-brained. And you *can* do it."

"Of course I can," Diana said. "It's perfectly natural, darling."

The little automobile moved along parallel with Kings River near the picnic grounds. On this Sunday afternoon five big picnics were going on—with music and dancing—Italians, Greeks, Serbs, Armenians, and Americans. Each group had its own kind of music and dancing. Spangler stopped the automobile at each group for a moment in order to be able to listen to the singing and to watch the dancing. "Those are Greeks over there. I used to know a family of Greeks. That's the way they dance in the old country."

The car moved on a short distance and stopped again. "Those people over there are the Armenians. I can tell from the bearded priests and the lively kids. That's what they believe in—God and kids." The car moved on and stopped near another group. "Those people are Slovenians and Serbs, and maybe a few other people from around in there."

The car moved a short distance and then stopped again. "Italians. Corbett himself is probably over there somewhere with his wife and kids."

Now, the automobile came to the last group. The music was loud swing, jive and boogie-woogie, and the dancing was wild. "Americans! Greeks, Serbs, Poles, Russians, Mexicans, Armenians, Germans, Negroes, Swedes, Spaniards, Basques, Portuguese, Italians, Jews, French, English, Scotch, Irish. You name it. That's who we are."

They looked and listened, and then the automobile slowly moved away.

37. Ithaca

THE AFTERNOON SANTA FÉ passenger train from San Francisco stopped at Ithaca and nine people got off, among them two young soldiers. But before the train moved on, a third soldier, with a limp in his left leg, got off and walked away, moving slowly.

The first soldier looked at his friend and said, "Well, brother, this is Ithaca. This is home."

"Boy, let me look at it," the second soldier said. "Just let me look at it." Now he hummed the delight he felt. "Ummmmmmm-man! My home, Ithaca! I don't know how

you feel, but *this* is how I feel." He got down on his knees
and began to kiss the brick of the walk again and again,
like a Moslem bowing to Mecca.

"Come on, man. People are looking. You want them to
think soldiers are crazy?"

"No, I don't, but I can't help it. Boy, my Ithaca!" He got
up at last and took his friend by the arm.

At length the two boys came up the street where Mr.
Ara had his market. Suddenly they began to run, one boy
running up onto the porch of one house and the other up
onto the porch of the house next door. Alf Rife came running around one house and stood on the front lawn
between the two houses, watching. The front door of each
house opened at the same time. The women who opened
the doors embraced the boys at the same time. And now
men and boys and girls and women took turns embracing
the soldiers. But there seemed to be a mistake. Alf Rife
discovered the mistake and began shouting at the top of his
voice.

"Wrong boy," he shouted, "wrong boy! It's Danny
Booth, the neighbor's boy! He's come home. He lives next
door. Came to the wrong house. We thought it was *our*
boy. It's Mrs. Booth's boy. There's our boy over there kissing Mrs. Booth. Wrong boy, Ma, wrong boy!"

"Oh, hello, Danny," Mrs. Rife said to Danny Booth.
"We thought you were Harry."

"Oh, that's all right, Mrs. Rife," Danny said. "I'll go
over and kiss Ma, too. You come over, too."

On the porch of the other house Harry Rife said, "Hello, Mrs. Booth. Come on over to our house, all of you. It
sure is good to see you, Mrs. Booth." He kissed her again.
"Danny's over on my porch kissing my mother."

Now, the lawns of both houses filled with people going
and coming in a kind of happy delirium, while Alf Rife
shouted over and over again, "Wrong boy, wrong boy! He
came to the wrong house! He lives next door. Hey, Harry
—*here's* Ma! That's Mrs. Booth! Wrong house, Harry!"

38. The Horseshoe Pitchers

HOMER MACAULAY, his sister Bess, his brother Ulysses and their friend Mary Arena on a Sunday afternoon walk came to a lot of people standing in front of the Kinema Theatre, and among them Homer discovered Lionel.

"Going to see a movie?" he said.

"Haven't got any money," Lionel said.

"Then, what are you standing in line for?"

"Me and Auggie and Shag and Enoch," Lionel said, "we came to the courthouse park to talk to the criminals. Then, they chased me away. I didn't know where to go. I saw these people standing here, so I came and stood with them."

"How long have you been standing here?"

"About an hour, I guess."

"Well," Homer said, "do you *want* to see the movie?" He brought some money out of his pocket.

"I don't know," Lionel said. "I didn't have any place to go. I don't like movies very much."

"Well, come with us, then. We're only taking a walk, window-shopping. We'll walk around town awhile and then go home. Come on, Lionel." He lifted the rope and Lionel got out of the line.

"Thanks," Lionel said. "I sure was getting tired standing there that way."

As they walked, Ulysses stopped suddenly and tugged at Homer's hand. He pointed down at the sidewalk. There before the boy was a Lincoln penny, face up.

"A penny!" Homer said. "Pick it up, Ulysses, it's good luck. Keep it—always!"

Ulysses picked up the penny and looked around at everybody, smiling at his good luck.

They passed the telegraph office from across the street and Homer stopped to look.

"That's where I work," he said. "That's where I've worked almost six months now." He stopped a moment and then, as if talking to himself, he said, "It seems more like a hundred years." He looked far into the office and then said, "I think that's Mr. Grogan. I didn't know Mr. Grogan was working today." He turned to the others. "Wait here a minute, will you? I'll be right back."

He crossed the street and hurried into the office. The telegraph box in front of Mr. Grogan was rattling, but the old telegraph operator was not taking down the telegram that was being dispatched. Homer ran up to him and said, "Mr. Grogan, Mr. Grogan!" But the old man didn't wake up.

The messenger ran out of the office and across the street to the others. "Mr. Grogan's not feeling good. I've got to go back and take care of him. You go home. I'll be along after a while."

"All right, Homer," Bess said.

"What's the matter with him?" Lionel said, not even

knowing who it was he was talking about.

"I've got to hurry back," Homer said. "Now go along. He's an old man, Lionel, that's all."

Homer hurried back to the telegraph office and shook Mr. Grogan several times. He ran over to the water jar and filled a paper cup, then splashed the water into the face of the old man. Mr. Grogan opened his eyes. "It's me, Mr. Grogan. I didn't know you were working today or I would have come down long ago, like I always do when you work on Sundays. I was just passing by. I'll hurry and get the coffee."

The old telegraph operator shook his head, reached out to the telegraph key and interrupted the telegrapher at the other end. He put a telegram blank into the typewriter and began to type a message.

Homer ran out of the office to Corbett's on the corner and asked for coffee.

"He's making fresh coffee now," Pete, the bartender said. "Be a minute or two, Homer."

"Hasn't he got any, at all?"

"Fresh out. He's cooking a new pot now."

"It's very important. "I'll go back to the office a minute and then I'll come back here. Maybe by that time the coffee'll be ready."

When Homer got back to Mr. Grogan, the old telegraph operator wasn't typing the telegram that was coming over the wire. Again Homer shook him. "Mr. Grogan, they're sending a telegram! They're making fresh coffee at Corbett's. I'll have a cup here for you in a minute or two. Stop them, Mr. Grogan! You're not getting the telegram."

Homer turned and ran out of the office.

The old telegraph operator looked at the telegram he had been typing, and read again what he had typed so far:

MRS. KATE MACAULEY
2226 SANTA CLARA AVENUE
ITHACA, CALIFORNIA

THE DEPARTMENT OF WAR REGRETS TO INFORM YOU
THAT YOUR SON MARCUS . . .

He tried to get up from his chair, but the attack came again and he clutched at his collar. After a moment he fell forward to rest upon the typewriter.

Homer Macauley came walking into the telegraph office as fast as he could with a cup of hot coffee rattling in his hand. He came up to the old man and set the cup down on the table. Now, the telegraph box stopped its rattling and the whole office became very quiet.

"Mr. Grogan!" Homer said. "What's the matter?" He moved the old man back, away from the typewriter, to look into his face, and as he did so, he noticed the incomplete telegram in the typewriter. He read the words of the telegram, but refused to believe them. He stood as if paralyzed, holding the old man. "Mr. Grogan!" he said.

Felix, the Sunday messenger, came in and looked at the old man, and at the messenger. "What's the matter, Homer? What's wrong with the old man?"

"He's dead," Homer said.

"Ah, you're crazy," Felix said.

"No," Homer said. "He's dead. And maybe I am, too."

"I'll call Mr. Spangler," Felix said. He dialed a number on the telephone, waited, and then hung up. "He's not home. What are we going to do?" He went over to see what it was that Homer was staring at in the typewriter. After reading the telegram, Felix said, "It's not finished, Homer. Maybe your brother is only hurt or missing."

Homer looked at Mr. Grogan and then said, "No, *he* heard the rest of the telegram. He didn't type it out, because he *heard* it."

"Maybe he didn't," Felix said. "I'll telephone Mr. Spangler again. Maybe he's home now."

Homer Macauley looked around the telegraph office. Suddenly he spat, and then sat down, as if in a trance, looking straight ahead. There were no tears in his eyes.

Thomas Spangler drew up in his automobile in front of the telegraph office after the drive in the country. He sounded the horn and Felix ran out.

"Mr. Spangler," Felix said, "I've been trying to get you on the phone. Something's happened! It's Mr. Grogan! Homer says he's dead!"

"You go on home," Spangler said to Diana. "I'll be around later—but don't expect me for supper. Maybe you'd better go out and spend the night with your folks." He got out of the car and kissed her on the cheek.

Spangler hurried into the office. He looked at Mr. Grogan and then at Homer. "Felix, phone Dr. Nelson—1133. Tell him to come right down."

Spangler lifted the old man out of the chair and carried him to the couch at the back of the office. He came back and looked at Homer. "Don't feel bad, Homer. He was an old man. This is the way he wanted it to be. Come on, now, don't feel bad."

Now, the telegraph box rattled and Spangler went to answer the call. When he sat down in Mr. Grogan's chair he saw the unfinished telegram. He looked at it a long time, and then he looked across the table at Homer. Spangler telegraphed the operator at the other end, asking questions about the unfinished telegram. The telegrapher at the other end tapped out the full message again. Spangler asked the other operator to postpone any more telegrams for a while. He then got up and went to his desk and sat down, looking at nothing. His hand fell idly on the hard-boiled egg which he kept for good luck. Without knowing what he was doing, he tapped the egg on the desk until the shell broke and then slowly he removed all of the shell, looked at the peeled egg, and dropped it in the wastebasket.

"Felix," he said, "call Harry Burke, the day operator, 4241, and tell him to come right down. When the doctor comes, tell him to take care of everything. I'll talk to him later."

Homer Macauley got up, went to the typewriter and took the unfinished telegram out of it. He filed the carbon copy of the unfinished telegram in its proper place, folded the original and put it in an envelope. He put the envelope in his coat pocket. Spangler went to the messenger and put his arm around him. "Come on, Homer, let's go for a walk."

They left the telegraph office and walked two blocks in silence. At last Homer began to speak. "What's a man supposed to do? I don't know who to hate. I don't know what to do. How does a man go on living? Who does he love?"

Now, coming down the street toward them, Homer and Spangler saw Auggie, Enoch, Shag, and Nickie. The boys greeted Homer and he greeted each of them by name. It was almost evening now. The sun was going down, the sky was red, and the city was darkening.

"Who can you hate?" Homer said. "Byfield knocked me down when I was running the low hurdles, but I can't hate *him*, even. That's just the way he happens to be. Who does it? I can't figure it out at all, but the only thing I want to know is, What about my brother? When my father died it was different. He had lived a good life. He had raised a good family. We were sad because he was dead, but we weren't mad. Now I'm mad and I haven't got anybody to be mad at. Who's the enemy? Do you know, Mr. Spangler?"

It was some time before the manager of the telegraph office decided that since there was really nothing to say, it might be all right to try telling lies. "Well, I don't think the enemy is people," he said. "If people hate one another, it is themselves they hate. A man cannot hate others—it is always only himself. And if a man hates himself, there is only one thing for him to do—leave—leave his body, leave the world, leave the people of the world. Your brother didn't want to leave, he wanted to stay. He *will* stay."

"How?" Homer said. "How will he stay?"

"I don't know how," Spangler said, "but I've got to believe that he will stay."

"No," Homer said. "My brother's dead. He's dead, and all the rest of us aren't."

Now, they were walking through the courthouse park, past the city jail, to where horseshoes were being pitched.

Spangler knew he had failed, but he decided to try again, to keep trying—lies, truth, anything. "I'm not going to try to comfort you," he said. "I know I can't. Nothing can. But try to remember that a good man can never die. You will see your brother many times again—in the streets, at home, in all the places of the town. The person of a man may go, but the best part of him stays. It stays forever." But he knew it was useless, and he was embarassed. "Are you any good at pitching horseshoes?" he said.

"No, sir," Homer said.

"Neither am I," Spangler said. "Would you care to pitch a game before it's too dark?"

"Yes, sir," Homer said.

39. The House

THE LIMPING SOLDIER who got off the train which brought Danny Booth and Harry Rife home to Ithaca, began to walk around the town. He walked slowly, looking at everything, and talking to himself.

"There's the depot—the Santa Fé. There's the Kinema Theatre. The Public Library. The Presbyterian Church. There's Santa Clara Avenue. Ara's Market. And there's the house!"

The soldier stood staring at the house a long time. Then he moved on. "There's the courthouse park. The city jail with the prisoners at the windows. And two Ithaca men pitching horseshoes." The soldier walked slowly to the two men and leaned against the low picket fence.

Homer Macauley and Thomas Spangler pitched horseshoes in silence, not even counting points. It was too dark now for the game, but they went on pitching. Homer was a little startled when he noticed the soldier leaning on the fence. For an instant he thought it might actually be Marcus. He went to the soldier and said, "Would you care to *pitch* a game?"

"No, thanks," the soldier said, "You go ahead. I'll just watch."

"I don't think I've ever seen you before. Is Ithaca your home?"

"Yes, it is."

"Are you on furlough?"

"No, they've sent me home—for good. I got off the train a couple of hours ago. I've been walking around the town, looking at everything again."

"Why don't you go home? Don't you want your family to know you're here?"

"More than anything in the world, but I think I'd better go home little by little. I want to see as much as I can, first. I can't believe I'm here. I'll walk around some more, and *then* I'll go home."

The soldier went off slowly, and Homer noticed his limp.

"I don't feel like pitching any more, Mr. Spangler, thanks very much." And then after a moment, "They're waiting for me at home. I told them I'd be home for supper. How am I going to go into the house and look at them? They'll know Marcus is dead the minute they see me."

"Wait," Spangler said. "Don't go home just yet. Sit down here. Wait awhile."

They sat quietly on a park bench, not talking. After a while Homer said, "What am I waiting for?"

"Well," Spangler said, not knowing for sure whether he was lying or telling the truth, "you're waiting for the part of *him* that died to die in you, too—the part that's only flesh —the part that comes and goes. That dying is hurting you now, but wait awhile. When the pain becomes total, becomes death itself, it will leave you. It takes a little time. Be patient with it, you will go home at last with no death in you. Give it time to go. I'll sit with you here until it's gone."

Now, from the Macauley house came the music of piano and harp and singing.

The young man sitting on the steps of the front porch, the soldier who had come home to a town he had never before seen, to a house he had never entered, to a family he had never known—listened with fear, doubt, and disbelief. What right had he to be there? And yet he knew that he *was* home. Ithaca *was* the place of his birth. This house *was* the house he grew up in. The family inside the house *was* his family.

Suddenly Ulysses Macauley was standing at the open front door, pointing. His sister Bess went over to see what it was. She turned to her mother. "Somebody's sitting on our front-porch steps."

"Well," Mrs. Macauley said, "ask him in, Bess, whoever he is."

Bess went out onto the porch. "My mother would like you to come in," she said.

The soldier turned slowly and looked up at the girl. He spoke very quietly. "Bess?" he said. "My legs are trembling, and if I try to stand, I'll fall. Please sit beside me."

The girl sat down beside the young man. "How do you know my name? Who are you?"

"I only know who *you* are, and who your mother is, and who your brothers are. Sit close beside me, Bess—until I quiet down inside."

"Do you know my brother, Marcus?"

"Yes, better than I know anybody else in the world. Yes, I know him."

"Where is Marcus?"

The soldier handed the girl a ring. "Your brother Marcus asked me to bring this to you."

Bess Macauley didn't speak for some time, and then she said, "Is Marcus dead?" Her voice was hushed, not excited.

Homer Macauley came walking down the street. Bess ran out to meet him. When they reached the soldier she said, "He's come from Marcus. They were friends," and then she ran into the house.

"Tobey?" Homer said. "I thought I knew you when we talked in the park." He waited a moment, and then said, "The telegram came this afternoon. I have it in my pocket. What are we going to do?"

"Tear it up, Homer."

Homer brought the telegram out of his pocket and tore it up but he put the small pieces back into his pocket—to keep, forever. "Let's go in."

Homer leaned down, and the soldier took his hands and slowly got to his feet.

Inside the house, incredibly, the music began again—piano, harp, and the voices of three women.

"Let me stand here a moment and listen," the soldier said.

Ulysses came out of the house and took the soldier by the hand. When the song ended, Mrs. Macauley and Bess and Mary Arena came to the open door. The mother stood and looked at her two sons, one on each side of the stranger, the soldier who had known her son who was now dead. Sick to death, she nevertheless smiled at the soldier, and said, "Won't you please come in and let us show you around the house?"